Waking
The Woodboy

Waking
The Woodboy

Max Hafler

**Wynkin
deWorde**

2 0 0 2

Published in 2002
by

Wynkin deWorde

Wynkin deWorde
PO Box 257, Tuam Road, Galway, Ireland
Copyright © Max Hafler, 2002
All rights reserved

A CIP catalogue record for this book is available from the British Library

ISBN: 0-9542607-0-8

Typeset by Patricia Hope, Skerries, Co. Dublin, Ireland
Cover Illustration by R. Derham of a puppet created by Pat Bracken
Cover Design by Design Direct, Galway, Ireland
Printed by Betaprint, Dublin, Ireland

Wake

Once upon a time, there was a city that had acres of land for its breakfast every single morning, so greedy it was for the land, and changing and growing so fast, it barely knew itself from one day to the next. It was a city on the edge of an abyss, and it was called Edge City. It was on the edge of Europe, the edge of the ocean, and lots of people lived there on the edge.

It was a city on a fast flowing river, a swollen city, a city bursting its banks.

In a month of Two Blue Moons.

And in that city there was a busy street where people walked and lived. Crosscurrents of people who walked and lived between banks of glass and stone.

And on that street were those who played and sang for them. Lithe-muscled fire eaters blowing their plumes of flame into the air on dark nights; jugglers and clowns : mimes and singers and artists and beggars and lost-eyed drunks; and a man and his . . . Bollox!

This is not a fairy tale.

I have to write when Mal's not here. Mal must never ever see this, it'd make him mad so. Real mad.

Calm down Lar. He won't be back for a while. Who're yer

1

trying to fool? No one's goin to see this. They might they might so. Will not. I'll be burnin on the fires an mi memoirs with me . . . Makin a merry blaze.

Apple wood holly wood mahogany an balsa . . . Sturdy apple for the head an face. Apple arms an apple legs. Plywood for the chest, with a foam vest to give it shape like. Hard holly for the feet. Dark, heavy, African mahogany for the hips. Balsa to make the hands as delicate as birds. Black leather caps on every joint. An strings. Long strings greased with cobblers wax. Strings that stretch all the way to heaven.

First thing I saw was blue. Blue pools. My eyes are painted blue. That's why it was, like. Blue whirly pools.

That cleared, an I saw Mal's face like a friendly doggie starin down at me. He smiled an said, 'hello fellah' then he kind of slid away, an I got this kind of whirlwind look around our dingy room, as he screwed mi head on. Then it was gone.

Blackness. A hole like. Thingness. No Thing.

Then I was dancin in the street to the Diddlyeye. Well, I wasn't dancin, it looked like I was, an Mal's pullin the strings, an a small blondy kid come up to me an smiled. We were the same height, an he looked oh so young an squashy like he might do anythin at all, like he might be handsome or ugly or what someday, like he might save the world or go mad in a shoppin arcade with a machine gun, who would know, while my face was hard an set an firm with the great smile that means absolutely nothin at all, as I think now anyways. An his spongy hand came out from his long-sleeved jumper, openin an closin his fingers like a fleshy little spider an he said, 'Lo.'

Lo, like an angel.

Then there was nothin again.

An then it's night. I'm in the bag, an I hear the doorslam, an a big crash as Mal falls over a chair. Then the growl of the zip. I hear that. An I see a yawnin, gapin slit out into the room. A light bulb with a dirty paper shade, then Mal's bleary smilin face appears in the gap, his skin lookin like it's tryin to do a runner off his face, his eyes cracked with red.

'Come on with yer.'

An Mal puts his hand into the bag an picks me up like King Kong does with whatever her name is . . .

How the fuck could I know about King Kong? Don't be askin. Didn't I see it on the video? For a while there I was really obsessed with seein all films that made inanimate objects look like they was real.

An there are some things I just kind of know, I don't know how like . . . I just do . . . An won't you say, well hasn't Mal told you all about them, but I know things about Mal that he doesn't tell me. I see things from his past he doesn't tell me, an I know things I shouldn't know considerin the time I've been alive – if that is what it is – what I am like.

An sometimes I can see things.

Thing is, you see, I'm so alone . . . will you stop it with the boohoos? Who wants to be readin anythin ought to be read over a body? Nobody. That's who.

Anyways.

So Mal has me in his hand right? Then next thing is, I hear this cryin faraway, like someone shoutin for help from down the bottom of a hole.

Mal. A terrible moan. Next thing I know I'm in the bed. Mal's holdin me like he's the chocolate an I'm the fillin, his brown paw tight across mi chest. An I feel all hot suddenly. Not warm like, it wasn't nice. If I said it was warm you'd think it was nice . . .

I feel his chest, movin up an down. Like I'm on a raft on the ocean. An ocean of breath an bone an skin. An the breath was like it was the tide of the sea in an out, in an out, an I give in an I'm goin with the breath like it's pullin me, like it's kind of draggin me, suckin me into the world, an I don't wanna go.

3

It went on an on an on, an sometimes Mal would let out a kind of moan callin me into life, like it was his pain that was callin me. An a kind of rockin started, an mi arm thrashed across the pillow, an I tried to grab it with mi hand as if it could save me, like someone who reaches for a cloud when they fall out of a plane . . . but I could only hook it, cos I'd no movement in mi fingers then at all.

It got so bad I let out a cry myself. Mi first noise.

AAAAAAIIIIIIEEEEEEEEEEEEEEE!!!!!!

Mal was almost dead with the drink, not that I knew that at the time so. He never heard that sound. Which was just as well, cos I think it gave me time to get mi bearings, before I came out with the truth like.

An slowly, slowly, there's this kind of softenin inside mi little head, an in mi little chest. An a whole wave of feelins floodin mi little wooden body. I had this feelin that the eyes were workin, but I couldn't see anythin at first cos I was covered with the duvet. I suppose if I'd been alive like, I mean really alive, I would have suffocated an it would have all been over before it had started.

But I wasn't alive like that. When I say I was alive what I mean is I was conscious. Aware of things. It was like I had feelins alright, but they were feelin feelins that spurted up like a fountain inside, I couldn't feel anythin to the touch. I suppose what I mean is that the feelins came from the inside out, not the outside in.

An mi head was floatin an I felt like mi whole body was floatin like the nice feelin you get when you're polluted, an before the Demon Drink crunches your head in his mouth. This floaty feelin went on for a good while. An then suddenly, it was if I was flyin round the room, above the bed like. As if mi spirit was decidin whether it wanted to jump inside mi body at all, an was just givin the livin accomodation a bit of a once over before makin the final decision to move in. An suddenly I feel miself callin, 'Come on spirit, please let's do it, just for the craic like. Come back.' An it did. Like a dog to his master.

I wanted to move, but I was scared.

4

Tick tock tick tock.

I moved mi head just a bit. Nothin fell off, so after a bit I lifted mi left arm. It was real difficult. An in a few seconds, mi hand in the little white glove was right in front of mi face, an I said in a thin crinkly voice, like a kinda alien off the telly,

'Hello hand . . . ' Mi first words. Hello hand.

I just lay there then for a second, letting them two words sink in to mi little wooden head. An then,

'HELLO HANDY! THIS IS LAR SPEAKING TO HIS HAND!'

Before I knew what hit me, this big moan flew out from Mal's mouth.

Shite I thought, well no I didn't think shite, cos I'm not sure I knew the word shite at that stage. Then he moved his hand an mi body jerked back like a horse in a Western, cos he had a hold of the strings.

I lay there all tense, like a beast waitin for the moment to run. Mi whole body was tinglin an all I wanted to do was escape. Move. Be Free. But I wasn't able for it. Mal had hold of the controls.

In the end he let go of me enough for me to be able to tease his fingers off the wooden cross that he controlled me with. I got all the strings together under mi arm, an I slid off the bed onto the floor. *Crash.* I didn't feel anythin at all.

I looked all around. The moon was peepin in through the old curtains an made a channel of light across the table an onto the floor. O'course, I didn't know at this stage what a shitehole we were livin in. I didn't know we lived in a block of flats where all the losers of the town were gathered like, not at all. I didn't know a thing. It was just magic.

The two big old armchairs, the big table, the television set, an Mal's paintings on the wall. It was like some kind of enchanted cave. After a while I struggled up onto mi little wooden knees, an I drew miself up to mi full 30 inches. I swayed about a bit. Dizzy. Then I took mi first few steps. It was hard. I had to tell mi legs to move like, you move, now you move, you an now you. They were like wood, ha ha. An there was this tinkly sound of mi joints movin, an me draggin mi wooden cross behind me. When I told Mal about this later on, he said it reminded him of when he was a kid in hospital with pneumonia an he had to learn to walk again.

Slowly, very slow like, I tottered right across to the big red armchair, an then mi legs gave up an mi head crashed onto the soft cushion. Wrecked totally. Then I thought, that's enough explorin for the time bein an I hauled miself up onto the chair an got miself together.

I started thinkin. What was Mal goin to say when he found out about all this? Maybe he'd just think he was completely cracked an throw me away or somethin? Well I didn't think that, not exactly. I just felt a bit kind o'panicky, an maybe I should try an walk back to the bed, but even at the start I kinda knew like, that he wouldn't remember takin me to bed. Not at all.

I looked at the box on legs in front of me. Mi window onto the world. An then I fell asleep I suppose.

O'course, when I say I fell asleep, what I mean is I just went blank. My eyes didn't close at all. I'd no lids, see? Everythin just went black in mi head. I have this movin jaw, but Mal said he didn't put eyelids on me. He doesn't like to see them on a puppet. Don't ask why. Mal's just a fella who has these feelings about things an there's no discussin it with him or askin him to explain himself.

Then, next thing, out of the blackness, 'Morning, World!' mutters Mal, like he's just sayin it to be polite.

An he opens the curtains with this quick swish like a play's goin to start. But it doesn't get much lighter in the room. Outside there's this great big pillow of cloud over the whole place an some fella up there, God I suppose, is squashin it down over us so we'll never wake up.

Mal's chargin round the room like a mad beast searchin coats an pockets, mutterin, 'Fuck you bastard,' then finally he sits hunched over this plate of old cigarettes. For a second there I think he's goin to eat them. Then he starts gatherin all the unsmoked bits of tobacco together an rolls them into a paper. Lights up.

'Thought I was a goner there Lar!'

He spoke to me. He knows I can talk. I'm about to say how are ye, then he says, 'We've got to get our arses out there double quick if we want to eat today.'

An I realise he's talkin to me, but he's not expectin an answer. He's not expectin me to say anythin, he's just talkin to me cos there's no one else.

Poor bastard.

Talkin to me with no hope of an answer. He was talkin to Me, a Thing of wood an wire an cloth. An this great big smile on his beardy face went on like a light when he spoke to me, like he had to communicate to somebody, anybody at all, even me like.

He turned on the telly. Jesus what the fuck is this. Two Breathers who looked like puppets were sittin in a living room I could see was fake, even at this stage, an they were talkin on an on about how everythin was gettin better an everyone was doin well. While they were discussin the merits of sushi, Mal rushed round the room, threw a plate from his last night's dinner into the sink with a crash an a 'fuck it I'll do it later', then he picks me up, ever so gentle an lays me into The Bag.

That fuckin bag. Sweaty black plastic inside. Mal said later I could be forgiven for thinkin mi mammy was a woman called Nike.

Anyways, off we go into the town, an all I can say is it's a good fuckin job I don't get travel sick.

It's a bloody long way, an all I can hear is the growlin of animals as I thought, which later I found out were the cars an drills an lorries. Then slowly but surely there's less of that kind of a sound, an a kind of a babblin takes over.

People.

Couple o'times I hear Mal shout, 'How are yer?' an 'How's it goin'?' an 'What's the craic?' but he doesn't stop to talk to anyone like, he just keeps on goin.

How are yer? I'm grand. How are yer? I'm grand.

Then we stop.

'Here we are now, fella. Our little spot . . . '

An he unzips the bag, an I get mi first real sight of the street, an the River of People. The River of People that never stops passing.

Legs legs movin movin, like a forest of flesh.

An it's like a kind of explosion of energy right in front of me, an *it's brilliant*. There's just *talkantalkantalkantalkhowareye what'sthecraichowzitgoin*. An it's like all the people passin are puttin on a show for me! BANG! LIFE. THIS IS LIFE! An I've got to pretend like nothin's happened an I don't know what's going on.

Cos I'm a Thing. I'm a Thing, a Thing . . .

But there's this trillin inside me, rushin through mi whole wooden body. I wanna move I wanna join in.

LEEEETTT MEEEE IIIINN!

A small kid's starin at me.

'What you gonna do?' American.

Mal's face ignites with a smile bigger than the one painted on my face, like somebody's pulled his strings. 'When yourman is ready, he's gonna dance.'

'Does he rap?'

'He does not. Leprechauns don't rap.'

'What's a leprechaun?'

'Did you never see *Darby O'Gill*?'

'Get a life,' muttered the kid. Mal didn't hear it or pretended he didn't. Just kept his painted smile on him.

The kid's owners arrive on the scene, a man with a bright open face, content with himself, easy, like he's done everythin right, know what I mean like? His wife, intense an dark, smiles too. They all wear bright yellow padded coats, clean jeans an trainers. It's like they're all in a team or somethin. Like they've just been into a shop an bought the lot that mornin.

Mal turns on the tape recorder an I dance. He makes me dance. To John McCormack an the "Kerry Dances". Do I hate that fuckin song.

Tis not easy at first, just pretendin to be a lump of wood. You just have to let your joints go, know what I mean? Relax. I want to struggle an say I am not dancin to this shitey music, I have a

8

mind o'mi own like. But I can't. I suppose most of you Breathers have to do this most of yer lives, right, do things you don't wanna do, for money? How the fuck do you manage it?

Before long there's this big crowd gatherin round us, an they're all lookin at us.

At me. All lookin at me. Mostly people in the bright coats an cameras hangin around 'em, an clutchin maps, with tiny kids pointin an gurglin, an I start to feel really great, I start feelin like this isn't bad at all. It makes me feel real important, an then the song's over an all the people clap, an suddenly they start throwin things at us.

Shit shit shit, says I in mi head, they were only pretendin to like us let's leg it. But Mal jerks mi head up to his face an I see that he's smilin so it must be ok, an all in a flash I know it's money, money that's pourin into the bag. Don't know how I know, but I do. Makes me feel great like. I feel all warm cos I realise that Mal an me are a team.

'An' what's your name, young fella? Are yer here for yer holidays?'

Mal takes me for a walkabout, an talks to the little kids, pretendin he's me. He makes mi jaw move, an asks them their names an all that. I start feelin a bit hot at that moment cos I want to talk for miself, but I know that I can't like. He puts on this sad little oirishy puppety voice but they are all absolutely lappin it up like there's no tomorrow. Still, I suppose if they knew the truth an I said, 'Do you know how much I hate that fuckin "Kerry Dances" crap?' they wouldn't throw any money an we could all stay at home.

The crowd goes off to who knows where, an Mal plops me on this little seat he's made for me. The toadstool seat. It's like a toadstool but it has a bit of a back on it an a hook so I can sit upright. To be honest with you now it embarrasses me to think that I was ever seen like that in public. Lucky for me, nobody'll ever know mi secret. Except Mal, an he's not likely to tell anyone.

Not now.

Mal starts to rummage in his pocket, divin his handie through a hole in the sheepskin coat an down into the linin. Lucky for him, he finds himself a smoke. So while he puffs away, I get a real chance to look around at the street.

This street, there's no cars on it right, just loads an loads o'people goin backwards an forwards. Most o'them are talkin an smilin, an they meet people an then they talk some more. Some of 'em look like they're talkin away into their own hands. It seems a very happy place, but not a place where anyone would stop for long cos everybody seems to be goin somewhere. It's as if the talk is like glue that holds people together for a bit but it starts losin its stick an before too long, the current takes the people off in different directions.

On the other side of the street there's windows, loads of windows. An people go in behind the windows an come out with bags. I know at once they're shops, that the people are shoppin. Buyin things with their money, an I wonder whether they all did a stint at buskin like we did.

Mal hates it when you call it buskin. 'It's street performin',' he says.

Across the street there's more buskers. One's a crowd with dark skin an black moustaches playin golden instruments. People don't stop an look at them much though they sound pretty good to me. I even find miself at one stage tappin mi foot a bit. Still they're rakin in the money alright. I remember wishin I could dance to that instead of the "Kerry Dances".

Further down on the other side, there's this statue. Well, o'course it's not a statue at all, it's a fella the colour o'stone standin on a box. He stays absolutely still until some person puts a coin into his box an then he moves an smiles an waves at them, an tips his stone-coloured hat an shakes hands with them. Then he's still again. On his box is painted the words, *"Nothing stands still forever."* Too right. Ha ha. An here's me to prove it.

I liked him. He was pretendin to be a Thing. Just like me.

The sun came out. An suddenly it was like it was the whole world smilin.

Mal finished his smoke an then it was time to get up again. He unhooked me at the back an up I went into the air like a kid on a swing. He turned on the music. This time it wasn't "Kerry Dances", but a song called "Galway Bay". An he didn't make me dance but moved mi jaw up an down to the fella singin on the tape. For a second or two there, I resisted like. Kept mi jaw tight shut, cos I thought – well I just couldn't do it like. But then the smiley crowds gathered round us again an I thought what the fuck it's grand. I love an audience.

The crowd was all melted away again an I was back on mi seat. All of a sudden I was starin at this dirty old pair of steelcapped boots in front of me, an this mangey slaverin black an white beast on a rope that looked like it'd have me for a snack. I let mi head fall back so I could see who owned the boots an there was this red face that looked like a car had run over it.

'Now then Philip,' says Mal.

An I feel scared like an I can't believe that my mate Mal would know such a deadbeat.

'I was home a few weeks back Mal, an' you know wha'? In London, you have to audition if you wanna go buskin' . . . ' the fella growls.

'Is that right?' Mal's nervy.

'Keeps all the crap off the streets,' an Philip puts a finger on to one side of his nose an blows, so that snot comes down the other an lands at my feet. The hound gets a bit of a snotty shower an shakes its head a bit.

People keep on passin an laughin like there's nothin happenin, an I see the dark fellas with moustaches an golden instruments are lookin across at us an startin to pack up their gear.

Suddenly it's like the whole world has shrunk to just Me, Mal, Philip, an the Beast. There's no one else on the planet. The street babble seems to fade away.

'I've only just started now Philip,' says Mal quietly.

An Philip looks down into mi bag an takes out a twenty. 'That'll do nicely,' he says an puts it into a back pocket. 'The street's a dodgy place to earn yer livin', Mal. You need a bit o'protection. Wouldn't like to see anythin' happen to a nice guy like you, would we? Nor your little mate neither . . . ' An he puts his filthy hand on mi little green head. An mi whole body fills up with red an I want to bite his hand. But I can't.

'See ya . . . '

An he strolls off down the street, toward some kid with an umbrella with bells hangin off it, who's gathered a big crowd round him, makin them all laugh.

'Fuckin' bastard . . . ' says Mal.

To make our losses up, we do another performance to great applause, an I'm thinkin Lar the movies await yer, when some fella with dreads lopes by – 'Hey Mal, howzitgoin', man?' – to ask Mal if he wouldn't mind lyin in a plastic bin liner as part of a demonstration against some foreign regime. Mal says he'll do that alright but I just sense he'll do nothin of the sort. An you know what's mad? The fella knows he won't do it either but he says, 'that's grand,' anyway. Then Mal goes beggy round the eyes an asks for a smoke off the man, so desperate it hurts me to see it.

An the fella who's called Budj gives Mal a smoke, an then swims up the river of people to the square where as many people as possible are goin to lie in plastic bags an save the world at four o'clock.

Mal turns back the tape an Fiddle de Dee an Diddlyeye it's back to the "Kerry Dances" again. Then there's this huge crash in the clouds an a flash, an water starts pissin from the sky an the River of People screams an runs.

Before I know what's happenin I'm being turfed into the air an back into the bag, an we're runnin too.

Is it us like, have we done somethin wrong? Panicky panicky. Don't they like the "Kerry Dances" anymore? Up down up down. Well that's grand cos I fuckin hate 'em. That's what I thought cos I hadn't a notion of rain at the time. Up down up down till we end up – yes, got it in one – at the pub.

The Pub. Mi first visit of many.

It was all seen through a hole in the bag where Mal hadn't

zipped it up right. That hole was like a round mouth, a vicious mouth with metal teeth.

An I had this flash that maybe all things were like me an had a voice an a mind an feelins when they felt like it.

An in mi head, I'm ridin up to Philip the Deadbeat on mi vicious Doggy Bag. Gimme back that twenty, I say. Fuck Off. Snap, the vicious Doggy Bag takes a big piece out of his leg. An suddenly Philip's shakin an quiverin an givin me the money. 'Here you are, Mal. Look I got the twenty back.' Then Mal says, 'Thanks Lar, you did a grand job there . . . '

But this was all a dream.

I was in the Heron pub. Mal was talkin to a fella I couldn't see, tryin to decide on tea or a pint.

For Mal this was not a simple choice like a 'what do I feel like at this moment' kinda choice. One pint usually meant settin sail on a black foamy ocean in a leaky boat with no life raft an no compass. An a feelin that he may never feel dry land underneath his feet ever again. An the voices. I heard them callin him in his head from over the boozy sea.

'Come on with yer, Mal. Come to the Land of Smiles, where everyone's content, yet the shadow dances. Come on, come to us. Let us stroke your hair an care for yer, while the tide tickles yer toes . . . '

An this mate of his, with the rubbery *threepintstaken* voice says, 'Go on Mal, you'll have a pint, so . . . '

'I won't Ger, now. I had enough last night.'

Ger smiles an says, 'Come on you will. Barry? Pint o'Guinness for Mal.'

So Mal has a pint.

Then another.

An another.

An he's laughin an smilin an sayin how this summer's goin to be a great summer, an everyone's laughin. *Whoosh.*

Out of the bag I come, an before I know it like, he's makin me dance on the bar, between the glasses. Jesus I am so happy. I am so happy that the smile is painted on mi face cos I don't know

13

how I could have kept it up like, cos I could see the frozen smile on their faces like, the *fuckinhellisn'tthisjustwhatalways happenswhenhe'sthreepintstaken* look.

An they've got no fuckin room to talk like, cos they have their own familiar voyages on the Sea of Drink. That smart-lookin woman there, she starts tellin the world that every fella's not worth the shite on her shoes after one. Yourman there laughin on the stool won't be long before he's pinchin every woman's bum an makin jokes that only he finds a gas. That jowly fella'll be steerin through the Straits of Despair after four, his face like a sad balloon after a kid's party. An that big man'll be callin you a bastard if you even look at him, an next minute, won't you be his best mate?

An this place, the Heron, kinda binds em together an it keeps 'em apart.

Anyways, Rubbervoice, who's just about to sink below the water line himself says,

'Will you take that fucking *paddywhackeryonastick* off the bar, before I knock it off?'

The words go through the air like a blade. Only the Diddlyeye goes on regardless. A young tourist couple look warily across at us.

Mal's whole body goes tight. Like he's frozen. Like a statue. He looks like he's gonna kill Rubbervoice.

Then he sweeps me up real gentle an lays me into the bag like a woman's dress. Mi head's stickin out of the bag so I can still see the happenins. 'C'mon Lar, let's go home,' he says. He calls goodnight to the barman, ignores Rubbervoice. He looks round the nook of the little brown bar as if every man an woman in there is his mortal foe.

Then out we go into the night.

I didn't know it at the time like, but those nights were important to him. The nights when he turned his back on the drink an the crowd. They made him feel like he was in control of things.

Mal pushes me down into the bag, an we're walkin over the

bitter bridge. Mal's walkin fast cos there's a fierce wind, not that I can feel it thank God.

'You know what Lar, there won't be a fuckin' blade o'grass between the city centre an' the flats with all this buildin' . . . '

An I don't know at all what the fuck he's babblin on about at the time. I'm tryin to think about how I'm goin to tell him I can move an talk. Wouldn't it be better like if he knew he wasn't talkin to himself at all, that I was listenin to him?

Then there's no wind an there's feet on stone. We're going up to the flat.

Bollox Fucker.

Fuck Off.

Younglads slaggin each other somewhere all echoey. An the slap of the feet on the stone gets slower as Mal gets tired an we get to the top.

Then there's the magic janglin sound of the keys. The door to our kingdom. It opens an I'm lowered down to the floor.

Here I am! Tis Me, yer puppet! I'm Alive!

I didn't say that o'course. I didn't know what the fuck to do. I was waitin for mi moment. Whenever that was.

The box goes on an there's some programme about animals called lions bein born, an their mammies teachin them to hunt, an I feel a kind of weakness. Then there's a hissin sound, a click, an water goin into a cup an the sound of Mal's arse goin into the cushion on the red armchair.

Sip sip. Then *Zzzzzip.*

Mal pulls out the stool an he puts me on it, so there we are, the two of us are watchin the telly. An I'm wonderin, does he know like? Would he have put me on to the stool to watch the telly if he didn't know that I could actually see?

Mal's eatin a sandwich. I'm not hungry miself. I didn't feel hungry at this stage an I didn't feel physical discomfort either, just kind of feelins inside that'd kind of drown me, which is just as well cos the fuckin toadstool was not what you might call arse-friendly. You weren't really sittin on it, it was the hook at the back kept you in place.

Still with mi big fat smile I looked happy as Larry on mi little toadstool.

Jesus there's a teapot chattin away to two cups on the telly. Things *can* talk.

An it made me feel all glowy an I looked as much as I dared around the room an wondered why all these things weren't pipin up. An seein these cups talkin made me want to talk so bad. I hadn't a notion of animation or computer graphics or animatronics at this stage.

'We did well today, you little star,' Mal says brightly, '83 euro even without that bastard's protection money. We'll be startin' you a fan club before too long, won't we? An' we'll be livin' in a penthouse flat, an' you'll be makin' movies. Lar in jacuzzi by his pool surrounded by Luscious Barbies, whaddyathink?'

Talk! Talk, you bollox! Can't you see he wants you to talk?

Then a movie came on, an there was a bit in it where this police fella fell in love with this girl who'd seen a murder, an he was touchin her an takin off her clothes, an next second they were in the bedroom an he was kissin her an lickin her breasts. They were kissin an he was moving on top of her an they seemed to be having a great time.

It made me feel a bit funny.

Then Mal had his thing out of his trousers, sighin an groanin as well.

'Beautiful . . . yeah . . . '

I wonder if he'd be doin that if he knew he wasn't on his own.

At the time I wasn't sure whether the two in the film had got him goin, cos their business soon faded, an before you knew where you were like, they were runnin through streets, being chased by fellas with guns. But Mal was still goin, 'oh come on come on beautiful.' After a little bit he seemed all finished too an he fell asleep in the chair.

Here was my chance! Mi whole body was trilling. I was gonna risk it, I was goin to stretch mi legs.

I unhooked miself from the stool. I gathered the strings together under mi arm an started to walk.

I had a good look round the telly. Magic. But if we lived in a place where a bit of wood, cloth, glue, leather an string can come to life, then this place must be full of miracles. How could people go about their lives like, with such wonders around? Gas.

I walked over to the window an looked out. It was gettin dark an all the lights of the town snaked their way into the bright centre. An against the dark blue skyline were these great monster metal birds like herons lookin as if they were pickin at the city.

'Joey . . .'

Mal groans in his sleep – first time I'd heard the word *Joey* which didn't mean a thing to me then – but shite fuck shite! I rush across the room to get back to the stool, then crash, as I go flyin over mi fuckin strings.

Mal wakes up, sees I'm not on the stool.

We both stay absolutely still. What else is there to do like?

Mal can sense things. He felt somethin was different. He was waitin to see what was goin to happen. What seemed like the whole day went past, then Mal lit a cigarette. The talkin teapot was back on the telly.

Nothin happened. A new film comes on. Mi whole body's full o'the excitement, but I still don't move.

If I speak, then things'll never be the same again, there'll be no goin back like, but then somehow I know that it's him that's brought me to life an so why would he mind if I just started speaking to him? *Whaddya want? Will you be able to keep your mouth shut forever?* You will not. You've got to talk. You've got to.

An then I hear this boomin voice inside mi head that says, 'YOU ARE A THING. THINGS DON'T TALK.' Made me feel the world would fall to bits if I talked. An lots of other feelins went whirlin round an through mi head like mad birdies. On the telly there was this grand-shoot out goin on, but in our room there was nothin an everythin happenin.

Mal cracked first heh heh. He lit another smoke. *Suck puff.* That went on for a while an I'm still lyin there not darin to move.

Mi ear's to the floor an I can hear a man givin out to a woman in the place below.

Then I hear Mal stand up, an he starts walkin over to me. For a second there I'm terrified an think he's gonna tread on mi head, an sure enough I see his old brown shoe bang in front of mi face.

Then he picks me up all gentle like, an puts me back on the stool

An he stares at me. An waits for ever.

'How are yer, Lar?' he says real soft like.

I'm gonna answer him. I will. I turn mi head towards him real slow. His own head moves back a little. His eyes grow.

'Grand,' I say, 'I'm grand.'

An for one of the few times in mi short life so far, mi painted smile fit mi feelins entirely.

No Strings

Mal's out. Great. On with the memoirs.

See, Mal is not like a normal fella. I mean, any normal kind of a fella would have gone fuckin hell I must be losing mi grip on reality, mi puppet is speakin to me, book me into a mad house, maybe I should give up the drink (not much chance o'that). But Mal is like a kid that way. He accepted it completely. More than that like. He loved the fact that I could talk an move.

He loved it.

Amazin I can still say nice things about him.

An he was no fool. We both knew right from the start that it had to be our secret, or in the end someone'd come an lock him up an throw away the key.

It was gas. Amazin really, when you have a secret, how much power you have, or think you have anyways.

It wasn't all easygoin like though, even at the start. At the beginnin, he treated me like some kind of a baby, no, more like I was a piece of paper he could write on. It took him a good while to see I had a personality, an I knew things.

One day he comes home with some stupid kids book.

'Why don't you learn to read?' he says.

I told him I could read already, that I didn't know how I could but I could like, an I didn't need to read about Jack an Jill or Three Blind Mice or Little Jack Horner or any such crap. 'Bring me *The Independent* or *The Irish Times*,' says I.

An then there was the food.

Mal was in one of his *lifeisfuckinbrilliantanmagical* moods one time, an he was rushin around gettin out the bowls an spoons one mornin. He grabbed me an put me on a chair with one o' the cushions from the armchair underneath, so mi face was just above the edge o'the table. He swept his hand across the front of me, so that the bits of food from the day before all fell like an avalanche on to the floor. Then he crashed a bowl in front o'me an he poured what looked like wood shavings in it.

'Will you eat?'

'If I ate that, it'd be the same as eatin mi own skin.'

He didn't listen. Then he poured milk on 'em. 'This is to make 'em delicious,' he says.

'I don't need to eat, Mal.'

'You need it to grow big an' strong . . . '

'I'm not goin to grow . . .'

It was like talkin to a piece of wood. An he doesn't listen an he's messin with the cornflakes on the plate . . . O'course I couldn't reason with him then, I wasn't able for it. I couldn't say, 'look man even if I did grow, what's goin to happen when I'm six foot three, an you're wantin to take me out in that fuckin bag an make a livin with me?'

See, he needed me as I was, as a puppet. Even then I realised it. Somethin he could control. Make me dance to the fuckin "Kerry Dances" an sing to "Galway Bay". What would he do if that all changed? As it had changed already?

From the very start, I had a personality crisis. I mean, the clothes like. Let's just zone in on the clothes for a second. I mean, I was not talkin like one of the fairy people, thanks be to God. I was talkin like a modern person. A person of Now. Know what I'm sayin? But when you're wearin the gear like, diddlyeye an *priceo'cows*, g'luck g'luck an *lookoftheweather* with a bit o'the Celtic Twilight thrown in for good measure is what's expected of a little fella in green. Follow me, for the Pot of Gold!

Clothes are fierce lablers. I mean, who sees a guard like as a person? An I was in those clothes every second of the day. There was no slippin into the casuals for me after we'd finished on the street. Only the green felt hat did I get to take off regular.

I had this feelin that I was neither a Thing nor a Human, that it was goin to cause a lot of grief like. An it did. You Breathers probably don't feel that very much. I mean, you're a Breather an that's it like, that's the story. You know just where y'are, but I didn't know. I mean, I didn't feel like a Thing either. I no longer had the companionship of bein a Thing. No Thing. I didn't have – I was conscious. But I wasn't a person. I wasn't even a cat or a dog or even one of the beetle army that came once in a while on a serious invasion, camouflaged by our curled up carpet that looked like a bit of old bread.

So Mal's mushin the wood shavins up in the milk. I wasn't hungry. I was scared an I didn't know why. I felt the hot feelin.

'Why don't you try it an' see what happens?' says Mal, like a mammy on a telly ad.

Crash. Sweep goes mi hand across the table an the bowl flies off the end, with the spoon chasin after it.

Crash. For a second there I see this hard look come across his face. Then it just melts away.

'Right so. You don't eat,' says Mal, an picks up the bowl, cleans up the mess. Doesn't say 'you fuckin bastard' or throw me across the room or anythin.

We made a deal. He fixed it so that when we came home after

work he could unhook mi strings. This was a bit difficult, as he had to put different types of hooks into me. I told him to work away like. It didn't hurt. I couldn't feel pain.

This wasn't true even at the start. I'll never forget him screwin them new hooks into me. I mean, it wasn't as if I could really feel anythin but there was some kind of a dull ache there, while he was doin it.

An then there was the bag, Nike. It wasn't like I needed the holes to breathe or anythin, but I just didn't like not being able to see things, so he made me a couple of spy holes which made the journeys to an from work a bit more bearable.

At the start like, I didn't complain about havin to dance or sing the stupid songs, cos simply bein conscious was enough to keep me happy. Anyways, I didn't want Mal to think I was goin to be always complainin. But pretendin I was just a Thing an that Mal was controllin me – that was the hardest of all.

Once, when we were out like, I don't know what got into me, I started kinda dancin on mi own, an he was havin to pretend he was makin me move. YOU pretend, you fucker, for a change, I thought. It was gas, cos o'course I could do the movements a lot better without the fuckin instructions coming down from above. The crowds loved me an we made a fortune.

It was the first time I saw him go ballistic.

When we got home an I heard the tinklin bells of freedom, the keys that is, an the door opened, he dropped the fuckin bag on the floor with a bang.

'What's wrong, Mal?' I say, as I'm gettin out of the bag an start unhookin the strings, somethin he usually did himself.

An he starts givin out.

'I couldn't help it, Mal. It just happened.'

'Well, you don't let it happen again.' An he bangs on the kettle.

'Nobody could tell like, an it rained money on us . . . '

'Bollox,' he says, 'That was cos it was a sunny day. Everybody wants to give you money when the sun's shinin'.' He takes a drag into his mouth, like he's stabbin himself with the smoke.

'Yesterday you said people give you more money when it's pissin' down, cos they want to feel sorry for yer!'

'You must never do that again,' he says, like a pot with a lid on, 'or people'll see that I'm not controllin' you. Do you understand that? If people find out about you, terrible things might happen to you. An' me too.'

'Right.' Right, I'm sayin, right.

He was real upset. I couldn't stand seein Mal upset or hurt. Or angry. An that's all bein angry is like. Pain. It's pain you can't keep locked inside a minute longer. An then he goes on at me. He can't stop like.

He didn't make me cry, though. I never cry. I can't cry. Tis a part o'mi Thingness.

Mal can cry though. Oh, he can cry alright. Like the river. But only after the drink. It's like it goes in one hole an pours out from the others, an on a bad day it might even pour out from the hole it went into. Next mornin he doesn't seem to remember what happened at all.

In the early days, I told him once, 'Mal, you were cryin.'

His face went like a stone, his lips set thin an his eyes set sharp, like I'd stabbed him an he was tryin to bear it. I didn't ask again.

The Unspoken Law of Ssssh.

Am I makin Mal sound like a fuckin monster? I am. He wasn't, he was glorious. He was a gas man then. An Jesus did we have a laugh.

I couldn't cry but I could always laugh.

I was so jealous of you Breathers once. You know why? Cos your faces are like windows, showin your feelins to the world. O'course, after I'd been around a bit I started noticin that some people may as well have had the faces painted on 'em anyways, cos when no one's speakin to 'em, the face gets kinda set an you can almost put a sentence to it like. The face that says, "The world is a shithole" or "I'm livin' in a dreamworld" or "Don't mess with me or you'll be the loser" or "I really am the happiest person alive".

How are ye? I'm grand. How are ye? I'm grand.

People smile a lot, which is great like. I suppose. If people didn't smile then no one would ever be happy, cos you'd never speak to anyone. At least you feel you can speak to people if they're smilin, without gettin your faced smashed in. Usually. Yep. Even a fake smile is better than no smile at all. Better to have the Smilin Sickness, than to come down with Despairitis. As one auldone said to Mal in a pub once, 'God help us boy, when the country stops smilin' . . . '

But when you're smilin all the time, even when you feel like throwin yourself into the river, then it really hurts.

For a good while after I'd come to mi senses, Mal was off the drink, well, not completely off it, but for Mal he was off it. He just couldn't wait to get home, let me off the strings like a doggie off the lead, an talk an have the craic. I was the star of the show.

We were comin home once, an we go into a shop. *Ting*. Mal says somethin to the fella I don't catch, then I hear him say, 'The oldies are the best. It's for the nephew. He's down from Sligo,' an the bag opens. He drops this box into the bag, an he whispers to me, 'You'll like this . . . ' An there on the front is this kid all made of wood. *Zzzzzip*. I can't see anymore.

PINOCCHIO.

Well if I could have cried when I saw that film, we would have been totally drowned. An the two below, who were always givin out to each other, would have called in the plumber. Pinocchio was my story. Well, it wasn't my story exactly like. But it was about a puppet that came to life, an the fella who made him was old an had no children, an the puppet got put in a travellin show an – well, I'm sure you've seen it yourself like. But I'm tellin you, the feelin I had while I was watching that film . . . The scariest bit was when Pinocchio went off to save his Daddy an the Great Black Whale reared up out o'the ocean an swallowed him down.

24

Many a time since, I've wished I had a conscience watchin out for me, even if it was only a fuckin bug in a top hat.

Mal had downed a few small glasses of the brown stuff by this time an he was sobbin away for the two of us, I thought. I climbed off mi little stool an onto his lap. He cradles me in his arms.

Then he says, 'Joey . . . Joey . . . '

See, there was one big difference between Pinocchio's story an mine, well two. The first was that there was no way I was turnin into a real boy. An the other one was that Mal had a son.

A real son.

O'course I didn't know Joey was a name. Hadn't a notion. I thought it was a word I didn't know. But it was like the cryin. *Unspoken Law of Ssssh*. I didn't ask cos I knew deep down that I didn't want to know anythin about it.

There was a picture of him in a black frame on an old chest. I'm lookin at it now. Under the picture there's a piece of reddy velvet, an a half-burned candle sits in a bowl next to the picture. It's like a shrine.

He was in a park, in the picture, an he had a smile on him so big, it was like his mouth was goin to fly off his face. He was feedin ducks with bread. An behind him there was a statue. That was a kid as well, tootlin on some kind of pipe, with lots of little beasts around his feet.

That smile. The little fucker couldn't have been that happy.

'I'm goin' off for a few days, Lar,' Mal says, a couple of days later over his wood shavings. 'Do you wanna stay here or come with me? If you come, you'll have to play dead, know what I mean?'

'Where you goin'?' I asked, a bit nervous. The idea of goin away an playin the Thing for days didn't thrill me, but then I didn't fancy the idea of bein separated from Mal. I was scared. Scared that maybe as it was his pain that called me into the world, that without him, well, I'd just go back into the blackness I'd come from an never come back, an I was enjoyin miself too much for that.

'My sister's. She lives up country. My little niece is gettin' First Communion.'

'First wha?'

An then I got this explanation about "The Church". 'O'course my sister doesn't really believe in it, but still . . . ' he says.

I thought it was a bit cracked to try an make your kid believe in somethin you didn't believe yourself, but I kept mi big gob shut.

'Are you comin'?'

'I will,' I said, still worried. Jesus, when I think about where we've been since like, with On-the-Tear Tours, I wouldn't have had a drop of fear in me.

Then there was this major lecture about not lettin on I could talk, an that we could only take the strings off when Mal came to bed. He also warned me we'd probably have to put on a bit of a show for the kids, or his sister would think he'd gone round the bend entirely, bringin the puppet with him.

I had to share Nike with Mal's clothes an a little toilet bag, which I used as a cushion. It was comfortable enough. As we walked along to the bus station, Mal's tellin me about Tara an her husband Mike.

'She's a city girl, my sister. But she married a farmer. She was so pissed off after a few months she got him to build her a breezeblock hacienda, in the hope she could pretend she was livin' in London or Dublin or somewhere. I don't think it really worked. An' now they're spendin' their entire lives payin' for it. The joke is, there's so many houses goin' up, if she lives long enough, the city'll come to her!'

Mal kept the bag on the floor by his feet while we were on the bus, but I got curious to see what was goin on.

'Mal . . . Mal!'

'Shut up!' he whispers. But I keep on goin. I want to see.

'Have yer an animal in that bag?' says this old woman's voice. 'I hope you don't . . .'

Jesus. Someone's sittin next to us. *Zzzzzip.* Mal takes me out.

'Holy God, now isn't that lovely?' says the old bag, but you can see in her eyes she thinks Mal might be on day release from an institution.

'I perform with him,' says Mal, rather grandly, in a way that only makes her feel certain she got it in one.

'Is that right?'

'I'd show yer, but there isn't room,' says Mal.

A little kid's face comes over the seat in front, 'God love yer,' says the auldone, but I'm just lookin out the window, tryin to act the Thing. An they're all chattin away, while I'm lookin at lakes an hills an mountains goin by, an even though the sky's a metal sheet, it all just looks so beautiful. So beautiful. Then this woman says that a fella in England . . .

'What was his name now? He had a puppet. He was very famous. But then the puppet kind o'possessed him. He'd give it things to eat, even sleep with it. It even had its own bank account . . . '

She cackled.

''Twas in the papers. That's carryin' things too far.'

An so, just to show the old biddy that no such thing could ever happen to him, Mal picks me up like a bag o'rubbish an stuffs me back into Nike. Then he smiles at the woman, an talks about the weather for a good while.

Zzzzzip. Here we are in the livin room, an the first thing I notice is how different it is to ours like. It's really clean for starters. Everythin has a place. There's so much light from this big window lookin out onto a lake. An it hits me that it's the first time I've been into another person's house. How we live is not the way everybody lives.

The whole family's smilin at me, well everyone but Barry, the biggest kid, who looks down his nose at me like I'm shite on his shoe. An Tara, Mal's sister, an Mike, her husband, they're not really lookin at me either, come to that. They're watchin Eoin an Emer, the two youngones, smilin at me. Only the two kids were smilin at me.

An I feel a bad feelin. A green feelin. Why is it that they only look at real kids with the soft look? Then I think, 'Don't be a bollox Lar, it's cos they think you're a Thing, that you have no life in you at all except when Mal's pullin the strings.'

I have the strongest feelins then to break away, an say, 'Hello, my name is Lar. I'm very pleased to meet you.'

I don't o'course.

Anyways, then we do the "Kerry Dances" an all that crap, an everyone claps except Barry. He just snorts, an goes off to his room to play some loud music before we're finished. After we've done, Mal sits me by the window, an they all go out an leave me to have the dinner.

The sun's goin down behind the lake, makin it all pink, an an arrow of birds passes an all them bad feelins sail away. In the front garden, to the side, there's another house, a ruin. Made o'stone.

They lived there once. Or maybe it was Mike the husband lived there.

I can see a fella in a cloth cap ridin a bicycle, an a young woman in a scarf an a long coat stands at the door of the cottage. It's not a ruin anymore. She's sportin a black eye, an her lips are pursed, like she has a frog in her mouth but can't let it out. A younglad goes by with a horse an cart with a pile of yellow grass on it, looks back at her. She slams the door. Bang.

Barry the Begrudger slouches into the room, ignores me an turns on the box. An there's loads o'smart rich yank kids, talkin about who's goin out with who, sittin around a swimming pool. An one lad gets a bit smart, an then a gorgeous girl loses it completely. She pushes the lad into the pool an all her mates laugh. They all laugh, except for the lad who got pushed into the water. When he gets out of the pool, even he laughs. Everybody pisses themselves.

Barry's got his hand on his thing. He wants to be like them.

28

Have those girlies draped around his swimming pool. With those eyebrows, matey? That fat hairy worm crawling across your forehead? An them cheeks like a volcanic landscape? In your dreams.

Then suddenly he's lookin at me, eyes snarlin. Like he knows like, what I was just thinkin. But he couldn't know. Could he?

Jesus. He stands up an starts walkin towards me. I'm thinkin, if I talk now, this kid is goin to have a heart attack. I'd love to scare the fuckin shit out of him. But I know I can't like. An I'm as scared as Pinocchio when he sprouts the donkey ears.

'How are yer, Barry?' says Mal, comin in.

Barry mutters, moves away, like he's been plannin a murder.

'Don't mess with him now, Barry. I need him for my work.'

'OK,' says Barry like he's doin Mal a big favour, as if to say, 'Well as it's you I won't tear the little fucker limb from limb. An' aren't you the saddest git on the planet to need a puppet to earn yer livin' . . . '

A bit later they're all sittin round the telly an the news is on. No one's watchin it except for the apprentice puppet killer, an the little lad. Mal's havin a large one an so's the sister, an the craic's mighty. I notice that the husband's drinkin tea. He's sworn off the drink, it turns out. He's a fair bit older than her. Great pools for eyes an a belly that says he's just about to say goodbye to his toes. An then Mal says somethin about Mike's dad havin died.

The air goes like glue, an for a second everyone turns into a statue. Mike leaves the room. Telly sound fills the space. Tara touches Mal's arm an whispers, 'Don't speak about Mike's dad, Mal.' An Barry looks across at them like he could kill him.

The woman I saw at the cottage, with the black eye. Mike's mammy.

'We don't talk about him.' Tara shakes her head, as if she's tryin to get a bug out of her hair.

Then Mike comes in as if nothin has happened, with little Emer in her Communion dress. 'Here's my little princess!'

'Isn't she gorgeous?' gushes the mother, suckin on her fag.

An the horrible atmosphere completely vanishes. *Pouf!*
Shazam!

Law of Ssssh.

As everyone is sayin things like you look like an angel, Barry
stares at the telly, which at that moment is showing thousands
o'people starvin on a mountain. But nobody sees it but Barry, cos
here we are in a different world.

Later on, Tara gushes away, with a *JesusMalifonlymammy-
andaddywasstillwithusnow*, an sobs gently till she goes
unconscious, an Mal has to waken her an carry her up to her
sleepin husband. Sobbin an the drink must run in the family.

That night I got a lecture about behavin miself, while they're all
in the church. Mal's really tense like, when he's here. I get the
feelin he wishes he'd never brought me. But I haven't done a
thing. He's snoozin away then, an I don't wonder that he's feelin
tense with Psycho Barry lurkin about.

'Come on now. We're gonna be late!'

Anyway they're all in the car ready to go. An I've already got
the strings off me, cos o'course I'm fully intendin to stretch mi
legs while they're away. The car starts, an I'm in the hall thinkin
about whether I'm gonna risk goin down the stairs, when little
Emer – shit shit shit! – comes back for somethin.

'Oh!' she says. Breathy little bird.

Shit. 'How are ye?' I say, an then I shoot back into the
bedroom. She starts climbin the stairs. Shit shit what next?

'For Chrissake Emer, do you wanna be late for Jesus?' yells
Tara from outside. The kid stands there for a second in the
doorway, just starin at me.

Play the Thing.

'Emer!'

She turns an disappears. I hear her runnin down the stairs an the door slams. If I could have heaved a sigh of relief, it would have blown a boat from one end of the lake to the other.

Mal said Emer had this mysterious smile on her face on the way to the church, just like she knew somethin they didn't know, an that Tara had noticed it, an said she was that inspired she'd start gettin mass again regular.

I clambered down the stairs, an went into the room with the telly. Facin me was the altar to the Family. The Fireplace. With the glowy fire in it you could turn on an off. It was all decorated with goldy figures an tools nobody ever used. An stretched across the altar were the pictures of them all. All the family had the jetblack hair that told you they had the sun in their blood. Only Mal though, had the tawny skin.

There was one o' the youngones when they were babies, an there was another with 'em wearing purpley ties an jumpers, massive smiles on em; a picture of Barry when he was small, smilin an lookin like he'd go to the shops for you anytime; an a recent one of them all in a foreign country with Barry starin out like his soul was full of the dark. In the middle of 'em, there was a picture of a thin Mike in a suit an a thin Tara in a long white dress. At the end there was a moody one of Mal, much much younger, without his beard, his eyes all sharp an twinkly, lookin out to the horizon like he was gonna climb a mountain or somethin.

An you know what was really mad? They all kinda looked the same, had a kind of stamp on 'em. I couldn't quite tell you exactly what it was like, but there was somethin. Somethin more than just how they looked. I remembered the night before, when Tara was slobberin Emer with a big kiss, she said, 'You have your Granma's eyes . . . '

It made me feel lonely that I'd never have pictures like that. An sorry for Mal, cos he didn't have many o'these pictures either. I don't know why it made me feel so bad like, cos all these pictures were just sad efforts to catch hold of Time, an at the end, all they was doin was remindin you that life was not all weddings, school

31

photos, winnin races, goin on holidays an gettin diplomas in flowy robes, an that Time was short for Breathers.

But not me. I realised then that I'd never grow old. That made me feel worse.

So then I pulled miself out of that pit, an decided to go out. I found a window open an I went out round the back o'the house.

It was a fine day. We'd be makin a fortune if we were buskin today. Whoosh. That thought just blew away. I was outside an alone. An I was so excited I thought, 'Fuck it I'm goin' round to the front, so I can get from under the shadow of the house, an see the lake.'

An I did.

Not a soul about. It was beautiful. I'd have cried if I could. Beyond the garden an over the road, there was a low green slope, an then the silvery bluegreen of the lake. So still. I felt like the whole world had its arms open wide just for me. An I opened mi little wooden arms to show the world that I'd take anythin he had to give me.

Not a wise message to be givin out, as it happened. But I didn't know that at this stage.

I felt so safe, yet at the same time real small – *I know I am small* – an I wondered whether people ever felt like this, even though they're bigger like.

I decided to explore a bit. I wanted to look at the ruined cottage. The rottin straw roof was all grown over, like the world had opened his mouth an was still eatin it.

I trotted across the short grass which was easy enough, an then through some spiky plants all laid out in neat rows, but then the terrain got a bit rough.

I was bein watched. Sure enough, glowerin at the gate, there was this beast of a dog with sad eyes an a log around its neck. It started to snarl at me, kinda half-hearted like, like it kinda remembered that's what it would have done for fun one time, but it had run out of steam, an was just doin it cos there was nothin else better to do. Anyways, I was still scared shitless like.

'Fuck off you bollox!' I shouted, not carin who would hear.

It turned an loped off slowly up the lane.

I climbed into the cottage. Inside there was an old table an a few chairs. An dirty white lacey curtains were still up at the windows hooked by briars. Mad.

In the small room, there was a picture of this fella with his shirt open, pointin at his heart. It was Jesus. I just knew it. What did it mean? Was he sayin, 'Look everybody, I *do* have a heart, like. Here it is for all to see.' ? I looked at this picture for a long time, an wondered why he had to do that. What was he tryin to prove?

I wondered if I had a heart.

There were other pictures of people in flowy clothes with lights comin out o'their heads. The whole place had the feelin of somethin that people wanted to forget about, but they couldn't.

An in the other room, there was newer things, black shiny bags o'stuff an tools. An from the doorway of that room, I looked into the big main room, an there was the woman with the black eye puttin a meal on the table for a small thickset fella who looked like he'd had more than was good for him. An a little kid –

Then it was gone.

I heard the car comin.

Shit shit leg it leg it Mal'll kill me! I'm out o'the cottage, runnin towards the house. But I'm still by the prickly plants when the car stops at the door. Lucky for us Mal gets out first, sees me, an falls flat on his face, pretendin to faint. I've seen lots o'girls do this in films on the telly, but never a fella.

It worked a treat all the same. They all gather around him –

'Barry get the door open, quick! Your Uncle Mal's ill!' says Tara in the kind of voice which tells you she thrives on emergencies.

– which gives *me* time to go to the back o'the house an climb in the window. I'd still never have made it, but the fucker Barry, King of Begrudgers, was so slow out o'the car an openin the door, like it was the biggest hassle on earth –

'Shift yerself Barry!' yells Tara. An Barry sighs as much as he dares to –

'Where's the key then?' he groans.

He puts the key in the door, while Tara an Mike pick Mal up. I can see their shapes against the frosty glass o'the door as I'm halfway up the stairs. An thankyou thankyou world, the key is stuck just long enough for me to get back into our room an flop onto the chair. I'm sitting on the strings, so I look like the Thing Incarnate.

They take Mal into the front room with shall we call a doctor an give the man a whisky an I'm fine I'm grand I don't know what came over me an Barry turn that fuckin telly off.

Emer comes into our room with Eoin.

'He can talk . . .'

'Don't lie. Not straight after your First Communion.'

'Hello,' she says, an this time I keep absolutely still. It would have broken mi heart if I'd had one.

She steps towards me, her eyes all confused like. I'm terrified she's gonna come too close an pick the strings up, see they aren't attached to me, an then start askin awkward questions below.

'How are yer?' she says softly, 'How are yer?' She goes downstairs with her little brother, almost cryin.

Mi big chance to turn mi whole life into a piece of family entertainment. Gone.

The house is still. I'm starin at the ceiling with mi lidless eyes. Below, Tara an Mal are alone, drinkin, tryin to reach across a gap that's wider than the lake outside.

'I'm worried about yer Mal, I tell yer. I'm worried about yer . . .'

'I'm grand.'

'Then why did you faint on the doorstep if you're grand? You're not eatin' right at the very least Mal. Look at you, you're a stick.'

'Thanks Tara . . . ' He pours a drink. *Glug.*

'You're not going to thank me for sayin' this,' she says, an there's a thick silence, an then off they both trot down a well trod road. 'Why you didn't just take over the shop, like Mam an Dad wanted you to, I just don't know.'

'You know why. Cos I'm an artist. I didn't see myself runnin' Fabric World for the rest of my life.'

'Some people might consider soft furnishings artistic,' she says.

'Not me.' *Glug*. 'Despite tryin' to groom us all for Fabric World, even young Martin didn't come back to run it. An' now, Fabric World, that emporium an' arbiter of taste an' fashion, is in the Great Shopping Mall in the Sky. An' so are they, probably tryin' to sell the angels some floral print cloud covers. Daddy was always a great fella for assessin' the market.'

'Don't speak ill of the dead.'

Silence. Then a small clunk as a glass is put onto a table.

'Well Mal, I can't pretend I understand you.' There's a bit of a silence but for the wind worryin the house, before Tara takes another few steps down *whatthefuckhaveyoudonewithyourlife* Lane. 'I mean, you're 44 years of age, Mal, an' what – I'm sorry to have to say this now, but it's just the way I see it – what have you got to show for it? When I look at what Mike an' I have got, I thank God. I really do.' A very loud *glug*.

Sigh.'When you're an artist you've got to make sacrifices. An' I fuckin make sacrifices.'

'I'm not an artist, thank God, an' I've made a lot of sacrifices miself, for this house an' the children. Mike an' I hardly ever see each other, with me workin' in the nursing home an' him on nights in town. Then we've a family to look after an' a farm to run.'

'Is it worth it?' Mal sounds weary.

'I wouldn't do it if it wasn't worth it,' she says, all tight.

Another silence.*Glug*.

'Have you heard from Joey at all?' she asks, with a kind of an edge, which I didn't understand at that moment, but it meant, 'an you fucked up your family as well'.

'He rang me just before we came away as a matter of fact,' lies Mal brightly, 'Things are goin' grand for him. I've promised I'll go across an' see him in the autumn, after the summer's over.'

Glug glug.

'Sure you gave up too easy.' says Tara darkly. Long silence an no *glug*.

'I'm goin' to bed,' growls Mal.

He was way too drunk to give out to me then.

Hi Diddle De Dee

'You thought I was dead but I'm not dead. I'm a real son, a flesh an' blood child, so I am. One day, I'm goin' to come back an' claim my daddy, an' you're gonna be thrown in the rubbish. You're gonna be chopped up an' burned on the fire the winos make by the river, to try an' keep their bloated hands warm . . .'

Joey started speakin to me. His picture did, anyways. I tried to pretend it wasn't happenin.

But mostly it was Diddlyeye an *Fiddlededeeanactor'slifeforme*, at this stage. I was havin a ball.

'Mal?'

'What?'

'Howzabout me havin a new costume like? I mean, this leprechaun shit, I mean, it's way behind the times like.'

Mal puts down his mug.

'What are you proposin'?' he says, with a highanmighty tinge.

'Well, I dunno.. sure you'd know that better than me. An' all this Kerry Dancin'. Jesus, doesn't it bore the tits off yer?'

'For one who's only been alive for a couple o'months, you're gettin' a foul mouth on yer.'

'OK. But will you answer the question?'

'Look,' he says, leanin towards me, 'we have to give the people what they want, an if they want the "Kerry Dances" that's what

36

we give 'em. Or we don't make any money. Aren't we making a good livin' as we are?'

We were. We were showered with money. We'd rehearsed so that I could do some o'the more difficult stuff on mi own, somersaults an all that kinda stuff, not that you could tell like, an people were just totally amazed. Course what this meant was that we didn't have to go out on the streets that much, which suited Mal down to the ground. I could have been doin it all day.

Truth was, Mal hated buskin. Felt it was beneath him like. Way beneath him. You could tell by the way he counted the money after the gig was done. Most times, he'd look down into Nike where the money was thrown, an leave it there till we was somewhere private. But if he felt desperate he'd look around to see if anyone was watchin, then he'd pick it up as quick as he could, scoopin the coins in his hands, lookin down at the floor, lookin anywhere at all as long as he wasn't lookin at the money in his hands.

Then came the worst bit, if he had to chase the coins that rolled on the pavement. 'There was nothin' worse,' he said, 'than counting your money in the street.'

He didn't mix much with the other street performers either. He'd hardly talk to them. You see, Mal was an artist. Mal was a painter.

Back at the breakfast table, the talk goes on.

'You know, a beautiful girl once said to me – she was a whore – do you know what I'm talkin' about?'

I did. Don't ask me how.

'You know what she said to me once? She said, "The great thing about whorin' is this: you never sell anythin'. You're not really givin' them anythin' for the money. Not unless you're a virgin. An' the great thing is, you can just sell it an' sell it an' sell it over an over again." An' that's what we're doin' with the

"Kerry Dances", Lar.' He grinned an supped his coffee again. 'So no hassle, ok?'

Let's see if yerwoman sings the same tune when her looks have fucked off an left her, I thought.

Cold. I felt cold all of a sudden. Inside. What happened to all the craic I'd heard at the beginnin, about the noble life of the street performer? Is that what I was then, just a way to make a bit o'money, so Mal could mash his brains out with the drink?

An I saw Mal on a tightrope in a circus high above the crowd. An then it was gone.

A brown envelope fell into our world. Mal jumped up, all excited. He was expectin it. He wiped his hands on his jeans, picked it up. 'This could be a change, Lar, there's a change comin', I just know it,' he says, a bit shaky.

I don't want a change. I fire a look at that little bastard in the photograph, an wonder if it's anythin to do with him.

As Mal reads he sinks down into the red chair. He sits there for what seems like forever.

'YOU FUCKING BASTARDS!!! YOU SHITES!!! YOU CUNTS!!!'

Smash. Cup against the wall – what have I done what the fuck have I done? He roars around like the room's a cage. I jump right off the chair an run behind the armchair.

'Bastards! Bastards . . . you fuckin' bastards . . . '

His rage melts.

He stands there now, in the middle of the room like, starin out the window, with this lost look on him, starin at the giant metal birds pickin at the innards of the city, then drops back on the chair, an covers his beardy face with his brown hand.

He's cryin now, just a low soft moan. It goes on for a good while. A good while. I'm scared to come out. He lights himself a fag. His hand's shakin.

'Mal?'

No answer.

'Mal are you ok?' I have a feelin now it's not my fault, but I can't be sure. He takes a few heavy breaths. He looks up at me an smiles slightly. I come a bit closer then.

Whoosh.

'We're gonna sort these fuckers out, once an' for all!'

He chucks me into Nike. In with the stool. In with the strings. *Zzzzzip*. Out the door. *Bang.* Walk walk walk.

'Mal, where we goin?' I say, tryin not to sound scared to death. He's gonna sell me to the highest bidder. I'm gonna end up with Mr Grimaldi, like Pinocchio did, an sit in a fuckin birdcage, watchin mi nose grow.

'Don't worry,' he says, 'be quiet now!'

'Mr Kenny, correct me if I'm wrong now, but didn't you sign yourself off the dole last year?'

'I did . . . '

'And become self-employed?'

'I made a mistake. It was a mistake.'

'But you earned just over the threshold last year . . . ' Kinda patronising *didn'tyoudowell* tone to his voice, 'which made you ineligible for the dole . . .'

'Sure, THAT was because I had an exhibition, an' I got a man, an agent, to sell my paintings. He made a lot of promises that came to nothin' . . . . But that was last year. I want to sign back on the dole like I was before, getting my weekly dole an my housin' benefit.'

'But – huh hum – as you know, your appeal has been rejected, Mr Kenny. That's the letter there in your hand, isn't it?'

'An' . . . an'. . . what does that mean?' Mal sounds shaky an weak all of a sudden.

'Well . . . hmmm . . . what it says I'm afraid.'

'If I don't get the fuckin' dole after the summer, I'll be homeless, an' I'm gonna STARVE!'

'Try not to upset yourself, Mr Kenny,' said the fella, soundin a little bit sheepish himself.

'Is it possible I can appeal . . . against the appeal . . . ' Beggy.

'It might be a long process.'

Mal's breathin heavy. In an out. 'Do you know what I'm doin' now? To survive? I'm buskin'. Wait, wait, I'll show yer . . . with this puppet.'

Whoosh. Lar rockets into bright world of grey furniture an strip lightin with lots o'desks an chairs. A man with a roundy face, grey hair an sad eyes stares at me. He's wearin one o'them polonecks, which makes his head look like it's been plopped on his shoulders.

'Now, isn't he a lovely fella?' he says to Mal, like he's speakin to a kid.

'He is all that's keeping me now from starvation.'

I don't know whether to feel sorry for Mal, or proud of miself, or both.

'What . . . um . . . does he do?'

'Sings an' dances to – Jesus what am I doing? What am I? –' Mal's lips tighten. He was talkin real loud like. Eyes screw up. Bang. Back into the bag. 'Look man, I don't want your sympathy, alright? I can't eat your sympathy!'

The man behind the desk goes puppety. 'I take it you declare these earnings?'

We're out on the street, earnin. There's no joy in it anymore. The joy's gone. It's like it's just desperate. The sun is shinin, but I'm not like. An all the kids are smilin. We don't stop for long breaks, like we did before, to watch the river of people flowin past. This is Work now. The whole afternoon Mal has a smile carved on his face.

On the other side o'the street, Philip an his dog are watchin us, waitin. Mal has a smoke, an Philip comes across to us for his cut.

'Fuck off,' says Mal.

Philip shakes his head, as if to say you'll be sorry.

A bit later, we were lyin in a pool o'blood.

We were just packin up when two of the deadbeats set about Mal an floored him. Lucky for me, I was already in the bag. It was still daylight in the full view o'the River of People, an no one did a thing to stop it.

'You should go straight to the guards,' said the lanky younglad, Brian, who holds a sign up all day further up the street, as he picked Mal up from the pavement.

'I won't. I'm grand. I'd only be interruptin' their cup o'tea.' An he smiled an laughed a bit, then started to cough.

'If you don't mind me saying, that kind of attitude is very old-fashioned,' said the younglad, 'You really should go to the guards.' Brian is hopin to make it to Cambridge University if his results are good enough. He's doin the job on the street dressed in disguise, with shades an a cap round the wrong way, an a padded jacket, so that no one will recognise him. This'd be normal gear for most young fellas his age, but Brian prefers shirts an ties. He thinks workin the street is for losers too. Just like Mal. But then Brian won't be workin on the street for long.

'Is that right?' says Mal, pretendin to agree with Brian, so he'll fuck off back to his sign.

We get home. Finally. Stoppin off for a half bottle on the way. Mal's dabbin his bruised face with a wet cloth. The news is on, an people are starvin, remindin us that things could be worse.

He takes a shot of whisky. No wonder you're always moanin about money, the amount of drink that's taken in this place I'm thinkin. But I don't say it. I say 'Ah well. Not the best day,' instead.

Then I have an idea.

Before the Golden Age of the Art Exhibition I'd heard about at the dole office, Mal had a reputation for reading them Tarot Cards. He still had the cards lyin around the place. People had said he was psychic an a wizard, an all that kinda craic. An some people had been a bit nervous of him like, cos he might hocuspocus 'em.

So this is what we did. Hee hee.

We knew where we'd find him. Philip an his beast would often sit with the other deadbeats by the river, smokin joints, dealin drugs an drinkin, laughin an wavin at suicides floatin out to sea, the kinda things you do when you're watchin the sun go down in a beautiful place. Sometimes, you'd see Philip there by himself.

Sun's almost down. Swans swannin. Visitors givin Philip an this guy Robbie, a big red whale in trousers, a wide wide berth. Blankin em out. They're on their holidays. They don't wanna see this kinda thing. Time ticks.

It's almost dark. Then there's just the two of 'em.

'There's whiiiiiisky in the jar . . .' sings the crimson whale, completely out of his tree, swiggin God knows what down his neck.

'Fuckin' shuddup!' jests the charmin Phil, an his dog growls, to back him up. Robbie falls back, grumblin.

Go go go!!!

'Jesus fuckin' Chriss shite shite!' screams Robbie, as I jump on his fat belly with a kitchen knife in mi hands. 'Don't hurt me . . . Jesus!'

Philip jumps up, staggers back.

'I'm not gonna touch yer, yer stinkin' pig,' I say, shittin myself if I could. 'It's yer master I'm after seein'.'

'Whaddya want?' says Philip.

'You had Mal Kenny beaten up a couple o'days ago. An he's sent me to tell yer that you'd better leave him alone!'

'Jesus that's really clever,' he says. 'Are you computerised, or what?'

'Mi Master has given me Life,' I say mysteriously, which wasn't far off the truth. 'He has a lock of yer hair, an he's makin a doll of yer right this moment, an if we have any more hassle from you, yer filthy bollox, you'll be dead in three days!'

'Come on Mal, come out now, or I'll step on yer little toy here,' cries Philip scratchin his head . . .

'An you'll die in the most horrible pain!' I shriek like a banshee. What a gas.

He aims a kick at me an I dodge it an laugh, 'I'm warning yer now. You have been warned!' I shout back from a safe distance, an run round a derelict buildin, divin straight into Nike, like she was the getaway car.

Out on the street next day. The swellin on Mal's face is kinda green.

'Why don't you paint yer whole face green?' says I. 'After all like, if I've gotta wear this fuckin green hat, I don't see why you shouldn't have a green face.'

We're workin, an suddenly I see the mean bastard leanin against the wall, smokin. Mal an me, we're circled by smiles, but all I can see is the hate an confusion beamin from Phil's dark eyes, an it frightens the shit out of me. Our set done, the crowd, our armour like, starts to melt. I feel very small. The smallest thing on the whole o'the earth.

Philip doesn't come over. He walks by. He looks scared.

That went on for three whole days. He just came an watched us. Mal started gettin bold, eyein the bastard back, matchin him like. I was scared to mi little applewood soles, that he was gonna misjudge the whole thing one of them days, an smile an say 'Howzitgoin' Phil?' or somethin. With a smart smile, know the kinda way? If he'd done that, I'm convinced he would have pushed Phil over the edge, an Phil'd be at us with a blade like, no messin. But Mal was no fool. Not that way. He said if you're gonna wake up somebody's demons to use against 'em, you have to take care, or the whole thing'll blow up in your face.

Then thankyou world or god or whoever did it, Philip an the beast completely disappeared.

We heard he was killed in a knife fight in Dublin. But the talk on the street, courtesy of Robbie the Red Whale o'course, was that we'd *hocussedpocussed* him.

Spooky huh?

I often thought about Philip's beast, that he was gonna travel cross the country back from Darkest Dublin to take revenge for his master, crack mi head in his teeth like a nut, then toss me into the river.

From that time on, the protection racket left us alone.

Beatin Philip, I felt a real hero, whether I really did it or not like. It was my idea an I'd risked gettin chopped up for firewood to do it. But somethin was startin to bother me. What was it we were goin out onto the streets for? Money, that's what. An what did I get out of it like? Absolutely nothin. I heard a fella say once when we were in BallyNowhere later on, 'A coin poisons the purest stream.' Country crap it may be, but tis true enough.

That's the time things between me an Mal started changin.

'Hello there, this is Mal Kenny. I'm afraid I'm not around at the minute. Leave a message and I'll get back to you . . .'

Beep.

'Hello Mal, this is Jan speaking. I hope everything's ok – I need to talk to you.'

We'd been out celebratin Philip's death. Mal had fallen over twice when we climbed the stairs to the flat, but he was in great humour till he heard the woman's voice. Then it was like Philip had come back from the grave an knifed him in the guts.

'Who's Jan?' says I. Law of Ssssh, Lar. I ignored the warnings completely.

Beep. 'Hey Mal, this is Brendan here. Can you help me hang an exhibition this week at the gallery? . . .'

'Good man yerself Brendan, a bit o'work . . . ' says Mal changin gear. 'I'll be there.' He turns to me with a faky smile, 'Brendan runs a little gallery in town.'

'Who's Jan?' *Law of –*

Mal ignores me, ranging around.

'Bitch. She thinks I'm gonna forget the kid's birthday. I'm not gonna forget Joey's birthday, Jan. There's somethin' for him in the post.' An he's shoutin at the machine. *'YOU FUCKIN' BITCH!!!'* Then he starts goin I'm sorry I'm sorry I'm sorry . . . an sinks into the chair.

'Mal? . . . '

'Fuck off! Leave me alone!'

An I start wishin I was still a piece of wood. Oh I'm great craic I am, sure. I can frighten away thugs an dance an sing an keep us alive an that's ok, but what the fuck *am* I? I'm Nothing me, I'm just a talkin thing. I've seen things talkin on the telly alright. You can make anythin talk with the right technology – That's me right enough, a fuckin interactive toy!

'You leave my daddy alone.' says the photograph. 'Fuck off yer little prick,' says I in mi head.

An Mal's rantin away. Then he gets tired. He sits down again. Turns on the box for company. But he keeps the sound low. He lights a fag.

Then he's cryin, an I want to go an comfort him but I daren't.

'How many times have I asked yer not to phone me, Jan? . . . what do you want? . . . I don't want to talk to you . . . Jesus . . . '

'Mal?' Talk to ME.

He looks at me, full of loss an hate. 'You just fuck off. What am I doin' talkin' to a fuckin' puppet? Talkin' to myself . . . You're not even real. A lie. You don't fuckin' exist.'

On the telly, a family's in a room that's gradually fillin with money, an they're washin in it, like they're playin in the sea . . .

'Is that right?' I say in a low voice. Mi mad head's achin. He ignores me. 'I said, is that right Mal?'

He ignores me again, so I start dancin an put on this stupid voice. '*La la la it's the Kerry Dancin . . .*'

He gives me a look that says Stop. But I don't stop.

Thud, Whizz. He kicks me against the wall an I go crash against the chest of drawers. Thank God I can't feel anythin.

I get up. I'm standin next to Joey's shrine. I thought Joey might be dead, but the little bastard isn't dead. I'm thinkin I'm goin to smash that picture, but I don't. I sit down again.

Then everything goes black.

'We should do great things today. The sun's shinin,' I say next mornin, tryin to pretend nothin has happened.

'We're not goin' out today,' mutters Mal.

'An why not?'

'I'm waitin' on a phone call.'

An I know the call we're waitin for is from Joey to say thankyou for his birthday present, cos today is Joey's Birthday. Mal finishes his pack of cigarettes by two o'clock, but he won't go out for any, in case he misses the call.

When you're waitin, the hours stretch like rubber.

We sat for a good part of the day in the dark. About three, the phone rang.

'Hello, How are yer?' Mal's voice high, a bit shaky.

'Mal, it's Brendan,'

'Hello there, Brendan.' *Crash*. 'I'll be there Brendan. Tomorrow, yeah. Who's the artist?'

Brendan tells him

'That bollox? Look I just don't like his work much that's all . . . Course I can still hang his paintings. I can still hang 'em Brendan. Amn't I professional? I'll be there . . . I'll . . . Sorry Brendan. I'm waitin' on an important call. Bye, bye, bye.'

Phone down. Face like he's sittin on broken glass. Twisty lips.

Beep beep. Beep bee –

'Hello?'

'Hello it's Joey.'

'How are you?' Mal's voice goes brown an soft with sadness an longin . . .

'Grand. That's right, isn't it, sayin' "grand"?'

'It is. Happy Birthday.'

'Thanks.'

'Are you havin' a good day?'

'Cool. Really cool. We went to Futureworld.'

Only the sound of Mal's breath an the buzz of the phone.

'D'you like yer present?'

'I'm –'

'What? Say it –'

'Not much into books,' *Tick tock tick*. ' But it's great.'

'You didn't like it.'

'No no. I *did*.'

'You said you were into the soccer . . . ' Mal sighs. Passes his hand over his face. 'How's your swimmin' goin' Joey?'

'I'm canoein' now. At Richmond. It's brilliant.'

'Ridin' the rapids, are you?' Mal's mouth quivers a bit. 'There's a spot on the river here like, where the canoers paddle upstream under the bridge. Everyone watches.'

'Oh, yeah.' The kid sounds bored. His mammy made him ring. Ha ha. Relief. Then just as I'm feelin better he says, 'Any chance of you coming to London?' The question poured down the wire an out through the hole in the phone right into Mal's ear.

Suddenly mi head's boilin.

'This year I promise, now.'

'You said that last year.'

'I promise . . . look I have to be goin' now, so listen young fella, happy birthday. Talk to you soon . . . Bye.'

'Bye.'

'Bye son.'

I was fuckin ragin.

It gets dark.

Cartoons on the telly, makin pictures on Mal's sad face. He has cans o'the black stuff an dives into 'em. I'm thinkin it's not a wise move like to show mi feelings, so I ask a question like one o'them carin interviewers on telly.

'That's Joey in the picture, isn't it?' First time I'd said his name.

'It is.' He drinks. Doesn't look at me. Stares at the screen.

'Where is it?'

'London. Kensington Gardens. We used to go an' feed the ducks. That's the Peter Pan statue behind.'

'Who's Peter Pan?'

So he tells me the whole story, fairies, never never land an flyin dust. Never takes his eyes off the telly. But he tells me everythin, as much as he can like.

'There's this part o'the story you see, that Peter'd hang around

Kensington Gardens hopin' to steal babies. Recruit them for the fairies. Joey was well fascinated with this. Oh, he really was like . . . He reaches out for the matches. Strikes one. Stares at the flame' "What would it be like if you could live forever? Wouldn't it be great to never have to grow up or get a job? Just fly around havin' fun?" I said to Joey, when we went there flyin' kites. Then he said to me, "But wouldn't it get so boring in the end? Everything gets boring in the end, that's what Mum says . . . " Which was absolutely right, cos she'd got bored with me alright.'

He turns his head as if the invisible Jan slapped him across the face. 'That's not fair Mal, not fair.

'*It is fair. It is,*' he whispers. *Glug.*

Tick tock tick tock.

'We dived into each other's eyes for pearls . . . Who am I talkin' to?' He breaks off. Drinks. Then his eyes look into mine for ages before he says any more. 'When I took Joey back that weekend, that was the first time I met David. My replacement. David shit fuck. His hand, it was like a sponge when you shook it like. Bland confident smile. Steady job.

Jan opened the door, really edgy. Usually at the handover we'd have a coffee or somethin', to show Joey we didn't hate each other, that we were grown up like. We went into the kitchen I'd painted, the burnt ochre an' ocean blue we'd argued about in the shop . . . David was out of place you could see. Way out of place. His jeans were pressed. He was goin' to get the two of them out of there an' carry 'em off to his own place as soon as they were ready.

David asked me lots o'questions, tryin' to be interested. Tryin' to be civilised, *no, no,* as if he was tryin' to find out what she'd seen in me to begin with.

"And what are you working on now, Mal?" he says, which made me feel like a piece of shit. Didn't mean to – maybe he did. Asked me had I tried illustrin' children's books?

No career guidance lessons right now thanks.

"Teaching? Teaching'd be a bit difficult, Mal's self-taught," says Jan apologetically. "How do you live then?" asks David like my father, incredulous that any fuckin' person wouldn't want to be playin' the shitey system.

HOW DO YOU LIVE??

MIND YOUR OWN FUCKIN' BUSINESS!!'

An Mal crushes the can in his hand, an throws it against the door. It dances a bit on the floor. Death rattle.

'Should have done that. Told him to fuck off, but I – "I'm a scene shifter in the West End . . ." I say like a wimp, like I was totally ashamed, like you could have scraped me off the floor.

Joey knew David. He knew him. Davo'd obviously been around for a while.

An I'm thinkin' wait a minute just a minute. "Were you around, Davo, when we were still together? Was all her talk about a bit o'space total bollox? *IT WAS, IT WAS TOTAL BOLLOX!*" I'm thinkin' that I saw his name an' a telephone number on the pad an' her sayin' somethin' about a driving instructor. An' I look at her then, an she knows I'm thinkin' this . . .

"That was another David, Mal, not him." Her eyes say to me. "You must believe me!" her eyes are pleadin'. "You must believe me, even though it isn't true, or else I'm nothing more than a bloody whore!"'

Another can gasps as Mal yanks it open. I daren't move.

'For a minute there I just wanted to snatch Joey up, run out of the door with him. Bring him back home. An' the very moment I thought that thought, you know what he did? He threw his arms round his mammy. So I ripped out my heart, threw it down the toilet, an' pulled the chain.

Ah well, I thought, I know when I'm beaten.

Joey puts his arms around me. Says goodbye. "See ya." Then off he goes into the front room to play with the computer game David's bought him.

As they go out, David puts his hand on Joey's shoulder. He put his hand on my son's shoulder.

Jan sits there. Beautiful long face like she's stepped out of a Pre-Raphaelite paintin'. "Well, see you in a couple of weeks then . . ." she says to me. There was something . . . Jesus . . . God, you know, she was almost cryin' herself! . . . an' she says, "You know, Joey needs you."

But what she wanted to say. *WHAT SHE WANTED TO SAY THE FUCKIN' BITCH! WAS GOODBYE! GOODBYE!* We're going to be secure an' happy an' stable an' normal like other people. *GOODBYE YOU FUCKIN' LOSER! FUCK OFF FOR GODSAKE AN' LEAVE US ALONE!*'

Mal has no friends, not really like.

Only me.

Only his wooden boy.

City

'"See Brendan, it was my kid's birthday last night. I was waitin' for him to ring me," says he. "He must have rung you very late," says I, "for you to not get in here till two o'clock."'

'That's Mal for you.'

We're in the Heron. Well, no, *I'm* in the Heron. In Nike, under a table. Mal's just gone off to buy some cigarettes. I can see four legs. Two apart an two together. An the fellas ownin these legs are talkin about Mal.

'If you can't take it, don't take it.' says Brendan, jeaned up legs an big cowboy boots shiftin, as he takes a drink.

'Absolutely, Brendan. You should know yer limit, alright.' says this whinin fella I've seen carried out of the Heron after abusin the barman on more than one occasion.

'So he starts workin' double quick time to try an make up for it –'

'Poor fella . . . '

'An' he's good, you know.'

'Oh, I know that now.'

'He's really good. Mal could go anywhere if he applied himself.'

Sup. Clunk on the table. *Sigh*. Heaven is brown wood an the clunk of a pint on the sky.

Then Brendan's hands go back to his knees. 'There's no generosity with him about it, that's what I can't handle. He fuckin' hates the paintings, so his heart's not in hangin' em.'

'He's jealous I suppose, Brendan, jealous of others' success.' sighs the whine overhead.

'I mean I don't love Baz McHugh's stuff myself,' whispers Brendan.

'Me neither – '

'But, I'm trying to facilitate the artist you know. Cos I've no axe to grind. An' I love doin' it.'

'You do, you do, Brendan . . . '

'An Baz's stuff, well it does sell. You've gotta have some exhibitions that are a bit more . . . well, commercial . . . I mean, a gallery's a business . . . I have a business to run.'

The door to the Heron opens suddenly an they both look around to see if it's Mal comin. It isn't, so they carry on talkin.

'An' Mal knows, he knows I'll tell him to fuck off home if he starts bitchin' about the paintings, an' I don't want to do that cos I do feel for the guy. I ask him what he's workin' on, try an' make him feel, well, valued, y'know –'

'You're a nice fella, Brendan. I hope he appreciates it.'

'– An' he tells me he's workin' towards an exhibition,' says Brendan, missin the compliment, 'which he's been sayin' since that fuckin' leech of an agent let him down after the one in my gallery.'

Sip. Clunk. Sigh.

'Then he starts talking about buskin'. "Street performin's a real art form," he says. How you can class dancin' with a leprechaun puppet an art form I don't know, but maybe I'm just bein' a snob about it. But I like buskers. They give the place character. Know what I mean?'

'But dancing with a fuckin leprechaun puppet, Brendan . . . Even the tourists wouldn't be falling for that anymore, would they now?' the Whiner sighs, an he rubs his little pasty hands together between his legs. 'Well, they would I suppose,' he squeaks with glee, an giggles a bit like a frothy drink. There's a flashy watch on his wrist, an the sleeves of an expensive jacket tumblin down his arms, an he flexes his feet in the neat pointy shoes. 'That's all very well for you,' I wanna say. 'What do *you* do for yer fuckin money? Bet it's not that fucking ennoblin. Whose arse do you lick?'

O'course I don't say anythin.

'"My puppet talks to me," he says. I said "Go way." an he says, "No really, Brendan, my puppet talks to me."'

I wanted to jump up now like a Jack in a Box, an scare the shit out of 'em.

'Now I know puppeteers an they do have a . . . well *a relationship* with their puppets, but he said it in a kind of way . . . I don't know.'

'How are yer, Maeve?' said the Whiner, to legs I couldn't see.

'An' he doesn't eat well. Maybe I should get the wife to have him round for dinner. Invite a few people over,' sighed Brendan.

But the little Whiner wasn't listenin. He was surfin on a smile, an chattin away to the legs I couldn't see. Then Mal came back, picked me up, an off we went into the street.

THIS IS A HARD-HAT AREA

The spot where we normally gigged an the river of people normally flowed was dammed up with cage, just lettin fast streams of people through on either side of it. Inside, machines an men dug up the road.

'Fuck me,' says Mal, 'What's going on?' he asks one o'the fellas in the cage.

'Cablelink. Telecommunications . . . '

'How long . . . ' A heavy drill starts. An old woman behind us tryin to get past says, 'Mother o'God.'

'Just a few weeks . . . '

'A few weeks?' yells Mal. 'This is the tourist season. My busy time.'

The fella shrugged as if to say what can I do like?

'Come on. We'll go further up . . . ' Mal was ragin.

We only got through the tape one time, then Mal just said, 'Fuck this, I'm not in the mood.'

I thought, 'You should worry, mate, you don't really have to do much these days,' but it made no difference. So he puts me in the bag with mi head stickin out of it, like I'm in the bath, an off we go.

We cross the old bridge. The river's rushin underneath us. We stop to look out onto the bay, an off to the Mountains of Somewhere.

Two foreign lasses lookin lost, are askin two young chancers where somewhere is. 'Well now, this is the old map,' says one o'the lads. 'You need a new map, came out a month ago.'

'Already out o'date!' chirps up the other lad, perched up on the lip of the bridge, an he laughs so hard he almost falls into the river.

I know what Mal's thinkin. He's thinkin about the people who've thrown themselves off this bridge. Quite a big crowd as it happens, all part of the *Unspoken Law of Ssssh*. An I'm thinkin Jesus, can we not think about somethin cheerful for a change?

A bunch o'gulls comes down onto the water to pick up fish, like feathery fingers tryin to pick up a pin from the floor.

'Sure, it's a beautiful day,' I quip, tryin to lighten the mood. 'We could have made a fortune on the street today.'

'Is money all you ever think about?'

'That's rich comin from you,' I thought. But I didn't say it. Cos I could see he was in pain.

I thought back a bit to when I'd come into the world, that his pain had brought me into the world, an I thought, maybe it's up to me like to cheer him up. An anyways, if I don't pull him out of this, I'm gonna be sucked in right along with him.

'Well if we're goin to stare at this lovely view all day, you might do better to look at that, instead o'thinkin about all the people who've tried to end it all.'

'How did you know that's what I was thinkin'?' he says.

'How are yer?' Some girl goes past with long dark flowy hair, an Mal's face goes on like a light. 'How are yer?' says Mal back. Her face goes on like a light too. Then it goes off. An she's gone.

We're walking up this little street of old houses. No one's goin by. So Mal's talkin away to me.

'That girl we saw on the bridge. Her name's Suzy. She plays the flute. Beautiful girl, don't you think?'

'Set yer sausage sizzlin, did she?' I asked. Heard a fella say this in the pub, without really knowin what it meant, but I saw 'em all smilin after he'd said it, so I thought it might do the trick an cheer Mal up a bit.

'I went out with her. She dumped me.'

Is there no end to this, no bottom to Misery Well? An if the truth be told now, I was the one who should've have been made miserable by mi own smart remark, on account o'the fact that along with no eyelids I had no thing either. But Mal had enough gloom for the two of us, an more.

'Where's this school then?' says I, tryin to raise Happiness from the Dead. We're lookin for Mal's old national school. I'm thinkin maybe we can crash the lessons, an give the kids a bit of a performance.

We turn the corner, an there's this little school. 'Where's all the kids then?'

Except that it's not a school anymore. It's offices for Chartered Accountants, whatever *they* are. Carey, Fitzgerald an Burke. Behind the offices is this huge crane, like some monster, dippin its long neck.

Mal sits down on a wall. Smokes.

'You can't live in the past,' I says, knowin full well there's some sad little story about stolen conkers about to start.

'They're ruinin' this fuckin' city. You can't turn round for a minute like without things are changin' all the time . . . ' he sighs.

An I open mi mouth to say somethin I saw on the telly about progress. Then I think better of it cos I know fuck all about progress an the efforts of civilisation . . .

Walk walk walk. A longish way. The watery sun drowned in cloud. Cold. Mal shudders a bit. Lots o'people walkin past with thin shirts on, huggin themselves, lookin as if they'd been betrayed.

'This is the house I grew up in.' chirps up Mal. 'I was born in that room.'

Stripey blue an green wallpaper –

Matching bed linen – AHH!

Breathe.

Everything ordered.

Breathe.

Little knickyknacks on the chest of drawers.

Holy God.

AAAH!!

An the little wildcreature that is now Mal takes his first thrash an scream in the world of Breathers. In this neat *everythininitsplacecolourmatched* world.

Tis a big detached house. Fabric World was obviously a goer from the start. I can see Felicity the mother, whirlin round the living room with a piece of beautiful red cloth held to her, 'God, I feel like Rita Hayworth!' she says, whilst this small kid, who, in the twinklin of an eye was gonna turn into boozy old Mal, paints pictures by the fire. All so cosy. Then I hear her sayin really sharp, like a hammer in mi head, 'Don't touch that!'

Don't touch that. I'd no picture goin with that like, just don't touch that.

'The house looks much the same as when we lived in it. Just different curtains, that's all. The new owners even kept the colour,' moons Mal. 'Bet they've no idea we ever lived there . . .'

Fabric World is now a building society. People queue up to get money from their accounts, to buy other things in other places. An you know what? Fabric World was on the main street just across from the spot where we always do our buskin. That's why we do it there. Cos Mal is givin his Mum an Dad the big "Fuck Off!"

Mal's lookin all wistful, rememberin, an I'm thinkin this cannot be healthy. I try to say somethin, but he just says when you've only been around for a few months you're not qualified to give an opinion.

'I wish I could grow up.' I say, tryin to be like Joey, lyin through mi little wooden teeth. Just to get some kinda reaction, you know?

Mal ignored me.

I wondered then whether all people grow up carryin these great slabs of despair on their heads, an if they *do,* no wonder there are stories like that Peter Pan, where it doesn't have to be like that. I suppose if you're a Breather, you've no choice but to grow up. I mean, stayin a kid is not an option unless you throw yerself off the bridge, is it like?

GROW UP OR DIE!

Jesus, I thought, I'm gettin as bad as the aulfella.

Off we go then, looking out for the secondary school. An there it is, a luxury hotel.

'I don't believe it . . . ' he whispers.

The Great God O'Blivion is callin him. The ship waits in the dock to sail the black ocean. Far away, the Harpies sing their soothin song . . .

Right now though, he's tense as a rod with a fish on the line.

'The whole fuckin' city's turnin' into an hotel!' he shouts an starts rangin around the fuckin car park, weavin in an out o'the shiny new cars.

'I MEAN WHAT IS HAPPENIN' HERE! YOU TURN ROUND AN' YOUR PAST IS GONE! GONE!'

A very large fella in a black coat comes out.

'Ok, ok Mal. Let's leg it now, eh?' I'm whisperin.

'Yeah, but who fuckin' stays in them?' he shouts at me quite openly in front of the fellah, who must think Mal has escaped for the day or somethin. 'Who has the money to stay in these fuckin' places?'

I can say absolutely nothin cos the fella's right on top of us, askin us to leave.

We're walkin back now into town, past a full graveyard. It's gettin dark. Mal, all hunched up like he has his whole life on top of him, is goin on an on.

'What's the point of livin' in a place, when yer past is just cut from under yer feet?'

'Don't live here then.'

'What do you mean?'

'Don't worry about it. I think we should travel. Why don't we go to America?' Put as much space as we can between us an that kid in England.

'What?'

'You'd make a fortune. *We'd* make a fortune. Yanks gobble up all this leprechaun shit. That, an sad Irish childhoods.'

'What do you know about it?'

'Plenty.'

'I'm not interested in money.'

'Course you're not.'

'Why do you think I am an artist?'

'An how do you buy paint an canvas an all the other stuff you need, without money? How do you eat? How do you drink? Course you're interested in money.'

'Are you my financial adviser now as well?'

God, bored shitless with our sad efforts to find a way out, sent the rain to shut us up. Mal walked faster. That was the end of the talk. The curtains of gloom were drawn.

I'd really like to have travelled o'course. But lookin back I know what I really wanted. Mal to miself. He might have made me alright, but he belonged to me as much as I did to him. I mean, I wasn't scared anymore that I couldn't exist without him. But we still needed each other. He was the only one that knew the truth about me. He was the only one that knew I wasn't just a thing. I was lonely. Lonely.

Joey. I fuckin hated that kid, even though he was far far away in Never Never Land.

'Fuck it,' says Mal. '*Fuck it!*' He turns away from the city, off to the open road.

'Where are we goin?' Panicky panicky. What now?

That was the start of On-the-Tear Tours. Courtesy of Mr Bendy, Mal's thumb. O'course, he'd only take care o'the travellin arrangements, an even then you had to be as flexible as Old Bendy was himself, but if craic an adventure was what you were after, then Bendy was yourman!

We stopped off at a shop, an Mal bought twenty fags an a bottle o'brown stuff. He took a big swig of it. I said, 'Fuck that's great. Amn't I the one who's gonna have to keep the head together –'

'Shut up, Lar, or I'll put yer head back in the bag.'

Then he stands by the road with his thumb in the air, like he was showin it to the drivers, "here look at mi lovely thumb" like. Tryin to look like he was the sweetest thing on two legs.

The sky went very dark, like it was almost night. 'Tis an omen,' I thought. An old grey car with one headlight, wearing his front bumper in a kinda casual way, slows down.

'Brilliant.' says Mal, pushin mi head into the bag. Where the fuck are we goin?

I was thrown onto the back seat like a sack o'potatoes. It was worse than the darkest corners of our place. I could see, through one of mi spyholes, beetles munchin on the remains o'two pieces an chips.

'Where you goin'?' said a deep voice that sounded like it ate grass. I undid Nike a bit so I could see what was happenin.

A weird young fella owned this voice. The back of his head was kinda pointy. His shoulders was massive. Let me out.

'Dunno,' says Mal. 'I'll tell yer when I've gone far enough. Is that ok?'

'Grand . . . '

Headlights caught the young man's face for a second, as he turned to Mal. He looked the spittin image o'Death in the Tarot pack Mal had at home, except for the fact that God had done him the honour of givin him a bit o'skin, so as not to frighten his parents.

'It's ok you know. You can talk to me. I've done some bad things in my time,' he says reassuringly to Mal. 'Got in all kinda scrapes.'

'Have you now?' says Mal a bit nervous with a big smile. 'Drink?'

'Don't drink anymore. Drink did for me. I won't.'

I really wanted to be at home that moment, watchin the telly, sittin in the red chair.

The rain started pissin down again. The wipers started real slow like they'd been wakened from a long sleep. Low rhythmic groanin.

'It'll stop sure, in a minute,' says the driver.

It did.

'I've done some terrible things in my time, so,' he says. Charmin introduction, eh? *His* time, I'm thinkin? How old *are* yer? You cannot be that old. These terrible things cannot be that long ago. But for him like, they were a lifetime away.

I felt something in mi little wooden chest, kinda thumpin. But it only lasted for a few seconds like, an then it was gone.

'In the town,' he says dark an slow. 'I'm blamed for everything. I'm tryin' to get my name back, you see, but people won't believe me. I do all kinds o'things, help my old neighbours, go to the shops for 'em, clean up, all sorts I do.'

Jesus. Stop the car. Open the door. This is some kind of a nightmare, like the start of a seriously bloody horror film. Sure, we'll end up chopped to bits.

The youngfella looked over at Mal, an said in a low dark way that'd chill your soul, 'Light me a cigarette, will yer?'

Mal gave him the lighted fag, and the Bones sucked on it to kill the Pain. The water fairly danced off the bonnet o'the car.

'People think I'm helpin' 'em out to get their land. 'Snot true. An' cos of my reputation, people are always tryin' it on with me, challengin' me, to get me into trouble. But I resist 'em. I do resist 'em. 'Tis very hard so.'

'Sounds terrible.' says Mal. The one light from the car reaches out onto the road like a man's arm drownin in a black river. The wipers swing like the pendulum on an old clock.

'I work on the trawlers now.' He had to tell us everything.

Jesus, that's it. He's gonna tell us some terrible secret, like where a dead body's hidden or somethin, an then, cos he's scared we're gonna give the game away, he's gonna finish us off an leave us in the wilderness somewhere. I bet yer this fuckin road is littered with corpses he's told this secret to . . .

'I have a lot of older men under me on the trawlers,' he glooms, 'givin' me loads of shite. Don't like to be told by a younger man what they should be doin', so they don't. But I like the challenge of it. I give 'em as good as they get.'

As good as they get? Sliced an gutted with the fish on the deck, no doubt at all! Where the fuck are we goin, Mal? Why are we doin this?

But you know what like? Mal doesn't seem worried anymore. He gets all gentle with him then. He offers him one of his own fags which the driver takes in his bony fingers, an starts askin him questions, the kinda questions the younglad might want to answer, kinda helpin him like. It's almost like Mal becomes another person. Understandin an carin, not like the interviewers on telly who are just kinda hopin the poor sod they're talkin to's gonna spill the beans about his sex life or break down, so that millions of people can watch an say, 'That's not me, I'm not like that.' Not like that at all. He kinda got onto the lad's wavelength.

His name was Ger. Ger's daddy was violent, beat the shit out of him as it happens, until one day he'd hit the dad an told him not to do it again. But Ger was always getting roarin drunk, an the whole family was already not liked in the town, cos of the father o'course. So Ger was always gettin into trouble. It was a pot waitin to boil over.

'One night, it was this fella's weddin', this fella I'd had trouble with in the past. I was in the hotel havin' a quiet drink on my own, when five or six of the bridegroom's mates came out into the bar in their suits an' all. One o'them had been sick in the toilet. It was all down his front. They all thought it was mighty, too far gone to know any different so, an' one o'them, the bridegroom's best mate, starts goading me a bit an' sayin', "Don't worry, that Ger O'Malley'll clean yer suit up for yer . . . " I said nothing. Then, tryin' to get a reaction from me, later on he said "You'll lick the sick off his jacket, won't yer?"'

The young fella's voice went all shaky as he went on, an suddenly I started feelin sorry for him. The rain stopped. The wipers went off. It was gettin dark.

'The cunt of a landlord turns to me, to me who'd said absolutely fuck all, an' says, "Drink up Ger, an' get out . . ."'

'An' did yer?' says Mal.

'Well I thought, "Fuck this I'm going nowhere," I said to him, "I'm gonna finish my pint an' then I'll go, but not before." Now I'd only had a couple so, I was not that far gone at all.'

I'm really hooked now, an I'm thinkin Jesus this fella is a great one with the stories.

'Then the landlord nods to the lads an' they started pullin' me out through the foyer of the hotel. Makin' a real show o'me. An old couple were shakin' their heads in the foyer as we went past. One of the bastards went off for Fahy then. He was the bridegroom.

The lads pull me out into the street. "Why don't you fuck off home," they say. "What do you think you're at, spoilin' some fella's weddin'?" But all this shoutin' it's just for show, just to make them look like they've been provoked. Cos they don't let go o'me, so I can't go home anyways. Then the best man Donnelly punches me hard in the stomach.'

He sucks hard on the stub of his cigarette. The burnin tip is almost touchin his lips.

'They knew I was a fighter like, I mean they knew how I was but they just wanted some trouble. I threw off the two lads holding me. They all laughed 'emselves sick, an' one of 'em shouts "Jesus the Incredible Hulk!"'

'Bastards,' hisses Mal.

'Well I tried to get away, even then I tried to get away . . .' an his voice went all weak for a second. 'But one big fat lad, Terry Newell, works in the hardware, thought it was all great craic, he stopped me. I punched him hard in the face an' he fell down. They all came for me then. I just went blank you know, I just went blank.'

'Smoke?'

'I will. Light it for me will yer?' Ger took a drag, an smiled a bit. 'Smoke too much. I'll stop one day, so I will.'

Low groan of the car. Back to the story.

'Next thing I know, I'm pinned to the ground. Then the bridegroom, he's over me, in his smart suit. He can barely stand himself. Then he laughs a bit, an' looks around quick to see who's lookin'. Then he kicks me hard in the kidneys. "Think yourself lucky I don't spoil yer weddin' chances O'Malley. I coulda done," says he, his face all twisted up. "Not that any hoor in their right mind'd want to marry yer!" yells the fat lad I'd hit before, an' they all go off laughin' to the hotel.

Nobody could stop me. Some o'them hung back they said, cos o'the look on my face. Fahy fell. His head hit a stone. He was dead before the ambulance came . . . '

'Jesus,' Mal whispered.

The rain began again. The wipers keened.

'At first the papers were full of it . . . The great local tragedy. Terrible. I was painted as the blackest devil in hell, an' John Fahy had the wings of an angel. Pictures o'Mandy the bride comin' out o'the hotel in tears. We got death threats to the house. Malicious phone calls. "We're gonna burn you out. You'll pay for this."'

I saw his shoulders rise an fall.

'It was terrible, for my mother, especially. They wanted me sendin' down an doin' for murder. But when the circumstances all came out, I got a year. Fahy hit his head on a stone.' He looked at Mal as if to say I have to believe this, or I can't stay livin.

There was a long silence. I wondered how many times the young fella had told this story. Maybe he just drove up an down the road pickin people up an tellin the story like a penance, over an over again, relivin it, askin for forgiveness. Like a curse.

'Why didn't you leave the town?'

'I wasn't goin' to do it. I couldn't, see? It's my home,' he says, all simple an dignified. Then he smiles a bit. 'Whenever somethin' bad happens in the area, I'm still the first one the guards come to. It makes me laugh now. But it didn't at first.'

'You're doing great . . . ' says Mal softly.

'Do you think so?' The younglad's eyes were all pleadin like. 'It wasn't my fault.'

'Listen to me now, will yer? I am very privileged to have met yer, do you know that?' says Mal in total seriousness, like a priest or somethin, givin absolution.

It just seemed such a perfect thing to say, at that moment. Ger's face broke into a little pained smile, like he was gettin forgiven by Jesus himself. What a perfect fella to be drivin us into the darkness, I thought. A cursed man.

Mal, I love yer.

I was still away with the fairies, watchin the grey wounded car splutterin off into the night, before I realised we'd been left in the middle of nowhere.

'Mal, where are we?' I asked, still a bit soft.

'I dunno,' sighed Mal shruggin his shoulders, takin another swig of his whisky. 'What does it matter?'

The spell was broken. *Smash*. Mal was himself again.

Absolutely what does it matter? Quite a lot to tell you the truth. We were by a forest. *In* a forest more like. We were officially in the Middle of Nowhere, an the Middle of Nowhere looks even more like Nowhere when it's pitch black an God an all the angels are pissin on you.

'Get back in the bag now, an you won't get wet . . . ' says Mal, an the soft feelin comes all over me again as I get in an zip Nike up.

Two cars passed us. By now it was really dark an there was no way like anyone was goin to stop for a wild beardy man in a wet coat.

We are in the wrong place, Mal. An Mal knew that alright, an yet he'd told the man to let us off here. Why does he want to be in the wrong place?

Thud.

'Mal? Mal are you ok there? Mal? Mal?'

I climb out of the bag.

Jesus he's dead.

64

Sidhe

They stared at us for a good while, saying nothin.

Shit, it's the fairies. They exist.

I heard soft pantings. Saw nothin. After Mal fell, I got miself outa the bag an came over to him to help him like. Then everythin went black an I fell on top of him, face down into his dampy coat. Like a grievin kid over a dead body. Lucky for me I was built to last in the wet weather.

'What'll we do?'

'Go back an get somebody.'

I saw miself at a fairy trial, an all the Silvery Beings were standin around me. They had me in the dock for fraud, besmirchin the good name of the fairies, dancin for the River of People, an being dressed like a bollox. Don't be a fool.

'Hello.'

The little girl turned me over with her booty foot. Round dirty face. Big eyes. Straggly bits o'blond hair comin out from her manycoloured hat. Behind her, the tall wooden fingers pointin to the sky. Is she the Queen of the –

Then the lad's face came. Wild lookin. Long black hair. Eyes like the pain of the world was locked in his head. An it was strange, cos they hadn't a notion I was watchin.

Mal started shakin an shudderin. Jesus he's not dead, but he is dyin. They moved back. Mal stopped. They both stared at us, not knowin what to do at all. The wildboy sent the girl off with a swing of his head, an she ran off . . . *squelch squelch squelch* in the mud.

Silence but for the wind. The boy looked at us for a long while.

'Who are you?' he whispered, like we'd come from another world.

Crows laughin, laughin their heads off at us, an the kid looked round like a wild beast, ready to run. 'Come on,' he said, through his teeth. 'For fuck sake, come on . . .'

Silence again.

Suddenly, a car was comin fast down the dirt road. The boy ducked down. Almost cryin with terror, he grabbed Mal's shoulder, an with his whole weight pulled him into the ditch. As he did this, I fell off Mal's body an rolled the other way, into the fuckin road.

Shit shit shit.

The car sped past. The wheel missed mi head by inches. Roar o'the engine, loud music an the snatch of a laugh. As they went by, they threw a hamburger box out of the window. It landed on top o'me. That's the fate of Things alright, I thought to miself. Use 'em an dump 'em.

The boy sighed. He turned Mal over.

'Over here. Over here, Gra!' shouts the little girl, Jade.

This big woman with red hair, wild like her head was on fire, took huge strides over to us. There was a round badge on her short green coat with a leopard on it, jumpin for the moon. She looked like a Queen alright. A big beardy fella an a thin little one followed Gra, with little Jade dancin before them.

'Did they see you?' asked Gra urgently.

'Don't think so. I pulled him into the ditch. It was hard but I think I was in time,' said the wildboy.

'Sure you were,' says Gra smilin.

Who were these people? *Were* they the fairy people Mal had talked about? In one way like, they reminded me o'people at home, but out here they looked kind of different, surrounded by an army of brown spears. It was like we were in another world entirely.

Magic. Bollox. Get a grip o'yourself.

Beardy Bone an Skinny Carl picked Mal up. The fuckers would have left me behind if it hadn't have been for Jade, who put me gently into Nike. Then she puts the strings in after me. A puzzled look lights her face . . . oh shit. She's wonderin how the fuck I got from the bag to Mal with no one there to pull the –

'Come on Jade, will yer . . . ' Wildboy's shout blew the thought away.

So off we went into the forest.

'Tommy, don't forget the kindling . . . ' I heard Jade shoutin.

We walked a good way. Nobody talkin but for the beardy fella sayin 'Are you ok, there?' to Mal, who groaned back. All there was, apart from that, was trudge trudge . . .

Then somebody starts playing a pipe. An I'm thinkin, 'Jesus we really *are* with the fairies. I mean, why shouldn't fairies say *fuck* just like the rest of us? Because they're fairies that's why,' an other such twisty thoughts looped in an around my head, which was just as well I suppose, cos it kept the panics away.

We stop.

'Don't worry puppet. We're nearly there now,' says Jade, smilin into the bag.

'Have you seen anyone?' The Queen's voice.

'Nobody.'

'Grand.'

'Who's this?'

'Jade an' Tommy found him on the road.'

'He's pissed.' mutters Carl.

'He's sick, Carl. He's been out all night in the rain with no shelter,' says Beardy Bone.

Carl snorts, cos he could have spent a week in an ice cold river, an still done a ten mile run . . .

'And look, he's got a puppet!' shouts Jade in triumph. *Whoosh*. Out I come courtesy of Jade's arm, an there's the encampment.

Where's the marble halls, an the bards with the harps, an all that craic? We're inside a kinda bowl of earth, where there's a few small tents an one larger one, an old van an a converted bus. Two or three dogs wander around. The circular mound has trees growin on it, which makes the camp hard to see till you're almost on top of it.

Four or five come walking towards us, including a stocky white-haired beardy fella who looked real fierce. He punched yer with a stare. Colum. He was the King like.

King Colum. Queen Gra.

'We have more important things for doing, than looking after drunks. We should have left him there,' says Carl.

It doesn't matter where you go like, there's shits aplenty, even in the fairy kingdom.

Colum decided that there was no need to panic, an that they could look after Mal for a couple of days. He had a fever an needed nursin. Besides, takin him to the hospital might create suspicion.

'Can I look after the puppet till the man gets better?' chirps up the kid. Everyone says o'course you can. So while Mal is put to bed in the converted bus, I'm taken off as Jade's prize.

I'm all alone in the world without Mal.

Little blue nails. Jade's mum had painted the nails blue on her little white hands an it was all chippin off. She held me to her stripey jumper an told me not to worry, that she'd give me back when mi dad was better. She seemed to have an instinctive grasp of the real situation alright

'You forgot the strings, Jade,' shouted Bone, as Jade an me crossed the encampment.

'He doesn't want them right now,' she says, an she couldn't have said a truer word.

She took me around the place. It did feel magic alright. The bowl we were in was kinda like a magnet for the earth like. I know you'll be thinkin blissy blissy, but tis how it was, so think what the fuck you want.

'Gra told me this is a fairy ring, and lots of fairies are buried here,' she tells me. Mal told me about bloody fairies an Peter Pan an I got the feelin fairies lived forever. But maybe that was English fairies.

There was two circular mounds, the one I'd seen already, an another round the outside of it. So when you walked between the two, it was like you were in a big ditch. On top of the mounds were spiky trees. We climbed up to the outer mound .

'I'll show you where we are,' she said, like a tour guide in the city.

Nowhere. Now it was official. Below us was a massive army of trees waitin for their orders. Further away there was great purply hills, like a serpent on the skyline. The silence sang in mi ears.

'You see all those trees? You're made of wood, just like them. They're your brothers an sisters.' Well . . . yes an no.

'Is that you down there, Jade?' A voice came from above. From the tower of a tree.

'Yeah. It's me, Gordon. Look I've got a puppet. He came with a man me an' Tommy found on the road. The man's ill. Gra's looking after him. That's Gordon,' she says to me. 'He's from Scotland an' he lives with us, with my mum an' me. He's not my daddy though. My daddy lives in Germany. Gordon's on lookout. Nobody must know we're here.'

She introduces me to everyone, an o'course I'm havin to play the Thing. They speak to me to humour the kid. I feel an eejit.

'What the fuck is this place, an when are we goin back to civilisation?' That's what I want to say. It's weird, so it is. Weird.

Is Mal gonna die? Will I play the Thing forever?

'Whaddyou want?'

Back in the ditch we met Tommy, listenin to music we couldn't hear, on headphones. Dancin jerky. Like a puppet. I could have laughed. Maybe some people in the world wanted to be puppets? He saw us, an he started like a beast, like we'd caught him rubbin his thing.

Jade said nothin.

'I'm only fuckin' listenin' to music alright? That's all. Fuck off. Can't you get any privacy round here?'

Jade's eyes filled with tears. I was mad.

'Sorry, sorry Jade . . . it's just . . . I'm not doing anythin', ok? An' take that puppet away. It's mad. Looks like it can really see yer . . . probably can. Bet it's just waitin' till we go to sleep an' then it's gonna murder the lot of us. Be in all the papers . . . "TRIBE MASSACRED IN FAIRY RING BY LEPRECHAUN."' And he laughed a dry mocking laugh.

I could have fuckin killed *him* that's for sure. I was thinkin maybe I could speak to Jade, maybe she . . . . See when you're all squashy an small like, you gotta think on your feet. I mean, o'course I didn't want Mal to die, but what if he did? Who could I talk to? An now I wasn't gonna be able to speak to her, cos if I did, she'd throw me on the bonfire double quick, thanks to this gobshite scarin her.

Cos I suddenly realised that without Mal, I couldn't talk. I was just a Thing. O'course I wasn't really. But everyone saw me as a Thing an so I *was* a Thing. Mal an me had made a deal for me not to speak to anyone else. Seemed the right thing to do at the time like. Out in the Real World. But here wasn't real, not to me anyways. Real was the room an the city an dancin on the streets. Here was a different kind of real.

An havin that secret, that secret that I thought made us so powerful in the world, the secret that I could actually move an talk, was in one way a fuckin massive burden, cos every time I told somebody that I wasn't really a Thing at all, I'd have to fuckin handle how they felt about it. You just never knew what they'd do. I was trapped in mi little wooden body. *Panicky panicky shit shit SHIT!*

'Tommy has no mum an'dad,' whispers Jade to me, walkin

away from him, 'He did a lot of drugs. Colum said he could stay
with us as long as he didn't take anymore. Except smoking a bit
of grass now an' again . . . '

I wondered what happened to you if you smoked grass. Still
they wouldn't run out. There was plenty o'grass everywhere.
Anyways, I wasn't thinkin about Tommy, I was thinkin about me.

Jade an me are at the door of the bus.

Mal's moanin an groanin inside, head tossin, body rollin. On
fire. I'm scared. What if he dies? What'll happen to me then?
Will the life drain out of me like water from a sink? You'll be a
Thing, you bollox, back to bein a Thing. I'm not a Thing
anymore. *What am I then?* What am I if not to have the auld
strings attached, an go dancin with Mal for the River of People.
Jesus, I don't want to be a thing anymore. I don't.

Mal screams.

Everyone looks towards the door of the bus. Holds their
breath, together.

'Is he gonna be alright, Orla?' Jade asks this young bit with
long hair, a purply top an long, dirty red skirt. She was sitting by
the bed an tryin to force this steamy green drink down his neck.

'Come on now, drink something cooling,' she says to Mal. The
green stuff trickles out of his mouth as Orla holds his head an
tries to pour it in. How can it be coolin if it's hot? The thought
flies through an away. Another thought flies in. Try whisky.

'I think he'll be ok, Jade . . . I don't know . . .'

It was almost dark, an the campfire seemed to be gettin brighter
as the time went on. The Tribe sat together, eatin a kinda stew.
They didn't talk much, an when they did, it was hushed. A dark
feelin was simmerin away there. I knew now o'course that these
were not real fairies, just in case you thought I'd gone completely
soft in the head like. I knew they weren't.

But they were.

'What if he dies?' asked the lovely Carl, breakin the silence.

'He won't die, Carl,' sighed Orla, with a bit of an edge to her. She pushed her flowy hair out of the way an mopped the last bit of her stew up with a bit of bread in her ringy fingers. Threw a look at Gra.

'How do you know?' meaning *whatthefuckdoyouknow-doctororla?*

Tommy put a log on the fire. It crackled an spat. 'Do we bury him in the forest, if he does die? What do we do? We should have left him by the road, like I said,' snarled Carl.

Orla sighed again. Took herself away from the fire.

Queen Gra looked mad, tossed her head like an angry horse. 'Jesus!' she said.

'What is it Gra?' asked Colum in this quiet way that said, it's ok, tell us. A bit like Mal was, with the young fella in the car.

'I'm sorry, it just makes me so fucking angry. I mean, we're supposed to respect life, aren't we? Isn't that why we're here? – an' here we are talkin' about leavin' a sick man to fend for himself.'

Mal starts moanin from the bus. 'Can I go, Colum?' sighs Orla. He nods, an she goes off to look after Mal, shakin her head an lookin back at Carl, really mad.

'I just think –' says Carl, like he's speakin from a great height.

'What do you think?' hisses Gra, walkin round like a beast it's unwise to mess with.

'Carl, Gra's right. It's unfortunate, I know . . . ' Bone tries to calm things down.

'I think we've more important things to be doing. Which is why we're supposed to be here.'

'Oh for Chrissake!'

'Chill out, Gra!' Bone tries again. 'Carl, c'mon now . . . '

Something flew overhead. A bat, a bird, or something. Only Jade an me saw it.

'I'm sorry but these are the decisions you have to make –' Carl went on.

'God, you are such a *wanker*!' boomed Gra. Her face went as red as her hair.

'Gra, that's it now, finished.' Colum's quiet kingness calmed her down a bit.

Orla, who'd come back out of the van when Gra started her heavy screamin, said, 'What does it really matter, what we're doing? What's it gonna change anyway?'

Then there was silence as thick as the dark beyond the firelight.

Twas never clear like exactly what it was they were supposed to be doin, except that if anybody found out about it, they would be so deep in shite that the whole of the Tuatha de Danaan wouldn't be able to get 'em out. That was the way they behaved anyways. It was a big enough thing alright, cos it was about savin the planet.

They decided to stay in the fairy ring for one more night. Only Carl voted against. He left the bowl of light the fire made, an walked off into the darkness.

After a while, Gra sang this sad tune with a voice that came from her heart an rang in her head.

An all of a sudden, they were the fairies again.

As the big fire was startin to tire of dancin, Jade an me went off to our bed . . .

'Don't worry, puppet,' she says. 'I'll take care of you alright.'

We lay together in her little bed on the floor of the van. Bone was singin outside by the fire now, playin a guitar. Gra sang too. Soft sound of drums.

The kid's love poured into me. An I wondered if she felt mine back. Cos that's what it was, I think. She loved me but she didn't need me, not like Mal. I so wanted to talk to the kid. But I couldn't.

Two darknesses ago, I was at home in the flat, watchin telly with Mal. I was fallin, Fallin.

Somethin happened while I was asleep, if that's what it was like. It was more than the blackness. Somethin happened then. I haven't a notion what it was.

'Mal!'

Shit shit, where the fuck am I? Shit. Conscious again. Jade asleep, turned away from me. It was still dark outside. A thirst on me. A terrible thirst.

All I wanted to do was drink. If I'd been at home like, I would have drunk the river dry. I had to drink. Cool liquid flowin down mi throat . . . *Coolcoolcool*. Like a river.

What's happenin to me? Wait till tomorrow. Wait till Jade pretends to give me a drink of her tea? No I can't, I can't wait. Jesus, help me. I'm so thirsty.

I squirmed out o'the sleepin bag an crept out o'the van. When I got out, I felt the night air.

Felt it. On mi face.

Over near the bus where Mal was on the other side o'the circle, there was a rain barrel, a rusty old-lookin thing. It was a long way off. I looked over the circle, lookin out for the dogs. Still a bit of glow from the fire. I started to walk across.

Squelch. Squelch. Giant stampin in the still night. Jesus someone'll hear me. What'll I do? I'm electric. I'm computerised. Won't work . . . Won't fuckin work . . . don't worry don't worry no one's gonna see yer . . . *squelch SQUELCH!!!* JESUS CHRISS! Keep going! They'll wake up! They will not! Will! Go back! You can't go back! *Squelch squelch fuckin squelch*! Don't wake up! Please don't wake up!

Grrrrraaah!

A surly dark beast with green eyes was watchin me pick mi way across the muddy circle. It stood up slowly, like it wasn't sure it could believe what it was seein. Behind the beast, a light was still shinin in a tent. Inside, two shadows made love.

I stopped near the embers of the campfire. Watched 'em, hypnotised like. A slow, tender dance. An you know what? They looked like puppets, Bunraku shadow puppets Mal told me about, from another country somewhere . . . *That* was what it was to be human. That was what it was to be *alive* . . . lovely . . .

The beast came forward, like a priest with a torch tellin me not to be a dirty bastard.

'Don't give me that,' I whispers to the dog. 'If the right one came along right now, you'd be ridin her, no messin.'

The dog snarled. Barked. The shadow lovers stopped, waited a second, an then started again.

Dry mouth. Liquid. Come on yer . . .

I made it.

The big orange tub by the bus. Lucky for me, there's a small ladder lent against the side o'the bus. I climbed a few rungs an leaned over. Lucky for me too was that the barrel was full to the brim.

Mi first drink.

I couldn't suck the beautiful cold water in, like you would yourself, I had to lick it with mi tiny wooden tongue, like a cat or dog. I could only take a little. Though I was dying o'thirst, mi whole mouth was sore like there was knives in it, but it was so soothin so soothin just another little sip sip sip . . . oh God . . . An the light did not really go on, know what I mean like? All I could think was that I had this terrible thirst on me an that was that.

'Where am I going?' cries out Mal from the bus.'Where am I going?'

Jesus is he never gonna get better? *Sip sip. Lovely.*

'Come back Joey!' He's cryin . . .

Joey, Fuck him. Little bastard.

Mal's whimperin an I can hear Bone sayin, 'It's ok man . . . '

Lap lap lap . . .

Tommy seems to come from nowhere. The eyes are bulgin out of his head like a Psycho. There's this huge smile on him like a big banana. He's walkin across the circle. He's gigglin. He has his headphones on an every so often he stops. Does some jerky puppet move. He sees me. He points at me an laughs. *Jesus.* He lurches across, catches me, an swings me up into the air. I try to play the Thing but he's not convinced an he starts dancin with me. I'm fuckin terrified. He's well out of it. What sounds like a band of mice from where I am, is boomin away in his head.

'Come on an dance! Come on an dance!' he sings to himself.
How do I explain? How did I get here?

'Come on an dance!'

Something's gonna happen. He's gonna drop me . . . Panicky.
Like I'm in a car with no brakes.

'Dance dance dance dance. Hey hey hey *hey*!'

One by one the others come out of the tents an watch. They
look well pissed off.

Jade runs from the van, really mad like. 'Give him back!'

Tommy stops dancin an looks with the stupid grin.

The kid controls herself, then holds out her hand real slow.
He's holdin me so tight. 'Give him back Tommy,' she says, like
she's in a cop film askin for the murderer to give her the gun.

He gives me back with a giggle. He says, 'He was off for a
swim in the rain barrel . . . '

'Don't be stupid.' she says.

Tommy starts dancin again an Colum comes behind him. He
turns him round and, holdin Tommy's face in his hands like a
priest holdin the magic cup, he stares into his eyes, just stares
right into 'em. Tommy's energy kinda drains away. The
headphones plink away in the silence. While this is pretty
spectacular to watch an all that, as soon as Colum lets go,
Tommy's banana smile returns, an he starts dancin again.

Colum sighs an moves over to Gra. 'You brought him here.
You take care of him . . . ' says Colum.

Gra nods an goes over to Tommy, an that's all I see cos Jade
an me go back to the van.

'That was an adventure now, wasn't it?' says Jade, as we get
down to sleep.

You haven't a notion.

As we was settin sail again for the ocean of sleep, I start tryin
to think what happened to me. I wanted a drink. Am I turnin
into a real human being? If mi body's changin, what's gonna
happen to me next? What does it all mean?

Bollox, this is all bollox. O'course I'm not goin to be turnin
into a real boy. Apple wood holly wood mahogany an balsa,

that's me. I didn't really feel thirsty at all. Just wanted to stretch mi legs, didn't I? Then I started thinkin about Tommy an how much he'd remember, then ahh down into the black.

Apple wood holly wood mahogany an balsa.

Early next mornin, there's a mist. Jade an me are awake before anyone, sittin outside in the clearin. I can feel the thin sun on mi little wooden face. All of a sudden a small brown thing with long ears nudges its way into the camp, eatin grass. Jade turns me to face her an whispers, 'Rabbit. That's a rabbit . . . '

Hop hop, nibblin its way into the centre. An everythin is so peaceful just then, me an the kid watchin this little beast, me sittin on her knee, her arm across mi middle. It's like a moment frozen in time, like it isn't long like, but it feels as if it's gonna last forever an ever.

Only it doesn't o'course, cos the black dog lifts its head an the rabbit sensin trouble, scoots back into the forest double quick. The black dog flies after it. An I wonder if the creature will escape an that we'll never know..

Then two people come from their tents. Slow swirlin movements, hands carvin the air an breathin deep. Bone an Orla stand in the middle of the camp, not lookin at each other, movin the same, breathin at the same time. Strokin the air like they're soothin a beast. Faces calm, set, but not set like mine. Lovely.

Will you listen to the little blisshead?

'They're doing their exercises,' whispers mi friend to me.

Then Carl throws back the flap of his tent, his face like he smelled somethin bad, an crawls out into the day. He lights a stove an starts to make the breakfast.

The others get up, an its like me an Jade are watchin telly. Then I thought back to the time when there was only me an Jade there, an how peaceful, how warm it all was, like the whole earth was holdin us, an tellin us not to be scared like. An how when the others got up, the air felt thicker an kinda went bad. The world's that way alright. The more people there are, the worse things get.

'Don't stay long now or you'll tire him out,' says Jade to me in the bus when we went to visit Mal. Truth is, she didn't want to leave me with him at all.

Mal looked a lot better. Better than he'd looked for a long time if you want the truth. Kinda smoothed out like, an his eyes were clear. 'I've had a great time with Jade,' I wanted to say. 'But I'm really glad to see yer, Mal,' I wanted to say. 'I think I might be turnin into a real boy,' I wanted to say.

But I didn't say anythin then. Cos Orla was there, an she wasn't for goin. Outside the bus there was this big meetin goin on about what the gang was all doin an what were they goin to do about Tommy, an Tommy was sayin, 'I'm sorry I'm sorry please don't send me away,' an, 'you are my family I have no one else,' an other sad things like that. Orla didn't want to be part of that meetin.

'It's hard to be in a group like this . . . it's hard to take responsibility.' she says sadly.

Mal was splashin around in her eyes. He took her hand. There was a long silence.

Jesus people change so fast, you can't turn round an spit but there they go, changin away . . . So he's gonna shack up with this Orla, an what's gonna happen to me then?

Fuckin hell, he's gonna kiss her.

Jade had left me propped up in a chair, so I pushed mi weight forward a bit an went crash onto the floor.

It worked. 'Pick him up for me, darlin'.'

'I'd like to do the runes for yer,' she says, after she picked me up an plonked me back upright, a bit viciously I thought, an I'm thinkin what kind o'mother would *you* be? 'Would you be into that?' an she gives him a blast of her green eyes, which I noticed she only did once in a while like, which o'course made the effect on Mal much stronger.

Mal said he would an he told her how he used to read the Tarot cards an all that craic. An she told him how the others had told her they thought she was psychic.

She pulls out this little bag with flowers sewn on it, an tiny shiny mirrors in the middle of the flowers. Mal shakes up the bag an then he pulls out these three little slabs, with marks on 'em. They lay 'em out on the blanket in front of him.

Bout half way through all this she says, 'Have you a son?'

'I do.'

'You don't see much of him, but your bond with him is very strong. Am I right?'

Mal's lappin all this up. Jeez didn't she sit with him all night when he was ravin? I heard him mention Joey's name twice miself.

'That bond's gonna get stronger,' she says, as she zaps him with the green eyes. His face lights up. I can see he's imaginin himself dancin with Joey an Peter Pan an all the fuckin fairies in Kensington Gardens. I'm like a bonfire inside me. But do you know what quenched that feelin? I read the runes different. I would turn into a real boy an Mal would claim *me* for his son. That was what was going to happen an that's what the runes meant.

'Orla, can you come out here for a minute, we need to decide something . . . '

Great God Colum's grisly face appeared at the door. Orla sighed, her head fell in a kind of obedience, which made her hair flop over her face like a stupid dog, an she went out.

Mal an me were alone.

'How are ye, Lar?' Mal's eyes were shinin.

'Grand. You look better.'

'It's the country air,' says Mal with a smile that says it isn't the air at all.

'The sooner we get back home the better,' says I. I don't really know why I said this like, cos I was lovin it there, but he looked all blown up with happiness, an I felt just then like puttin a pin in it.

'Ah you're a man for the city alright!' he says with a smile.

79

'What have *you* seen of the countryside anyways, shut up in the bus for the last couple o'days?' I say, smart like an kinda out o'mi depth. 'An listen to 'em,' Carl an Gra were givin out to each other again, outside the bus, 'What do we want with this *savintheworld* bollox? It's a fuckin waste o'time.'

'I don't suppose they'd agree with yer.'

'Jesus, they do nothin' but fight all the time.'

'People are like that Lar. You wouldn't know that o'course . . . '

'No, o'course not,' I says, real mad, 'cos I'm only a Thing, but what if I wasn't a Thing?'

'What?'

The voices outside get louder. Orla's sayin that Mal is still weak an can they not wait another day, an Carl's sayin Orla should get a job as a nurse if she likes carin for sick people, an Bone's goin 'Carl, that is really out of order.'

Orla comes in cryin, but before we could hear the result of all the arguin, Jade comes back for me.

'Jade, the puppet belongs to Mal. You should leave it with him now, ok?'

Jade pouts a bit.

'Say thankyou to Mal for letting you play with him.'

'Ah sure, thank *you* very much, Jade,' says Mal, with his big open smile, 'for takin' care of him while I was sick.'

'That's ok,' she says very quiet. An the kid gives me a hug an her love soaks into me. Then she turns away an runs out the door.

'She wanted to keep him,' says Mal.

'Ah, she'll be fine now. Jade's not into things.' Says Runewoman in a slightly *highanmighty* way.

I am NOT a Thing, Miss Not-So-Psychic Bitch.

Tis how I felt like.

'We have to get you up Mal,' she says with a sigh. 'Bone's comin' in to give you a hand.' She leans over his body the exact same way I've seen on the telly in the afternoons in black an white films to "help him" with the blankets – Jesus I am gonna puke! – an surprise surprise, he leans forward an starts suckin on her mouth.

80

What about me?

And there's this horrible hot bubble around 'em, like they're gone with drink cos nothin else matters, no one else matters. What you gonna say now, missus? "You seem to be getting your strength back right enough?" Is that what you're gonna say?

She pulls away, as Bone comes in the door, an the two of 'em get Mal out the bed. Orla ties the laces of his old black shoes, lookin up at him, sittin on the edge o'the bed tryin to smile an be brave for her, when his face looks like a piece o'bog paper that's been pissed on. Bone tells him to put his hand around his big shoulder, but Mal says it's ok an walks carefully to the steps o'the bus then takes each step one at a time. As he passes me, he winks quickly.

So that's why I've no eyelids. They're signals of deceit.

Outside, there was a bit of polite clappin like from the gang. While they were out I had a little drink of Mal's water by the bed.

'Now we can get on with the business,' snarls Carl outside.

We got on with the business alright. At night. One o'the worst nights o'mi little wooden life. There I was zipped in the bag – 'Don't worry I won't be fuckin comin out to watch anythin!' says I – while Mal an Orla,

'Again more aaaahhh'

All fuckin night. Jesus I was mad. Jealous. Jealous of everyone. Mal, Orla, Joey. Oh I was *really* jealous of him. Cos if I'd have been Joey right, Mal wouldn't have done this in front of him.

Just a Thing. I was just a fuckin voice in his head, wasn't I? Even though it was his pain brought me into the world. I tried to keep still in the bag but I couldn't like, I tossed an turned a bit, but it didn't matter. I could have got up an sang a John McCormack medley an they wouldn't have taken any fuckin notice.

Finally everythin went black. Hurray.

Cold air. Bits of light through the bag. The odd spit of the camp fire. The sound of someone suckin on a cigarette.

'Lar? You awake?' Mal's voice. The zip opens stubborn, like it can't be bothered. Light pours in through the bag mouth. I sit up.

We're still in the fairy ring. But they're gone. The only thing to remind us they were there at all is the burnt patch of ground near where we're sittin, a few squashed squares o'grass, an some muddy tracks..

'They had to go,' says Mal smilin softly, savourin the mystery an the *shipsthatpassinthenight* of it.

The Runemaiden's with 'em. Good. One enemy back to oblivion.

I clambered out the bag. Looked around, standin on the shiny lazy grass. An for a second there I wanted to say, let's stay here Mal, now they've gone, let's build a place an stay here forever. I can't even believe I thought a thing as soft as that, but I did so. I did. An o'course I say nothin o'the kind. Instead I say, 'What now?'

'Let me finish this smoke Lar, then we'll go. Is that ok?'

He finished his smoke while I listened to the birds, then I hopped back into the bag, this time with mi head peepin out the top so I could look around, an we left the fairy ring. We walked off into the trees, which were like this great big brown an green cathedral. I dunno like, I felt kinda sad, cos I knew somethin real big had happened.

One time I looked back, we'd only been walkin a short while, an already I couldn't see the mounds any more.

They were gone.

Forever.

No Place Like

I am not going to grow up. Things are gonna stay just as they are. *Unspoken Law of Ssssh.*

We were back.

We walked through the city. Early mornin the next day. The sun squinted on us. It was all quiet. Everywhere there was holes in the narrow street, like people were lookin, diggin, for somethin that was long gone. An the holes were decorated with this red an white tape flickin in the wind. As we walked up one o'the oldy worldy streets, this army o'hardhats appears from nowhere, an before you can say *whasthecraic*, the pneumatic drills start, an the big trucks an diggers are movin around like surly monsters in the street.

Home. I never thought I'd be happy to get back to that fuckin room but I was like. When Mal opened the door, I took a great run an bounced onto the big red armchair. As Dorothy says in the *The Wizard of Oz* . . .

Mal threw the half-eaten slice o'toast into the stinky bin. The rottin pack o'milk with green lips tumbled in after it. He put on the kettle. There was a thin layer of dust everywhere, as if God an the Angels were puttin a sheet over everythin in case we didn't come back.

At first, it was like the room was givin us the cold shoulder,

'Where the fuck have you been? Why didn't you take me with
yer?' it said. But slowly the moody room warmed up an not long
after like, me an Mal, we're forgiven for goin away an leavin
Room all alone. In the end, the walls of Room hold us tight, an
whisper to us, 'Please don't go away again . . . '

Beep.

'Mal, this is Brendan. How are ye? You are a hard man to get
hold of. I wanted to talk to yer about the gallery openin' up in
this new coffee place in town. They wanted some interestin'
pictures, I gave 'em yer name. They'll be contactin' yer . . . '

Mal looked at me, his eyes all fire. I'm thinkin that's a bit of a
comedown after the Age of the Great Exhibition an Big Promises,
to hangin a few in a new café, but poor aul Mal is too desperate
to be thinkin so proud, an anyway, maybe he's right. Maybe it's
better to show yer pictures in a fuckin shed than keep 'em under
yer bed, or worse still, not to paint at all.

He went to see "the space" – this is what Artists call it like – an
he comes back all fired up. It's like a cave he says. The light's not
that great but they've agreed to put spots on the paintings an
make a real show of 'em. He's got a month.

An all the gloom an doom is forgotten as Mal rises from the
ashes like a different person.

'I'm off the drink now, Lar, till after this exhibition,' says he.
Ho ho. I mean I just cannot believe him like, specially as the days
with the fairies were completely dry, 'Won't I be needin' the
money for paint an' canvasses?'

While he was out lookin at the gallery, as Mal calls it, or café
as I call it, I took mi first drink of creamy white milk.

'What's this one called?'

He'd pulled all his old paintings out from under the bed.

'It's called *The Guide.*'

It was a long paintin of one of them younglads in the street sittin on a little stool in front of a sign which points the way to shops. On one pointer it says, "Oona O'Dwyer, Beautycare", on another "Upwardly Mobile Phones Inc" on another "Frank Connelly – Funeral Director". The lad's got headphones on, an he's starin right out o'the picture. The eyes are big an empty.

There was another really scary one –

'Recognise him?'

Philip the deadbeat, now really dead, an his snarlin beast, with a dark alley behind em. In the doggie's slaverin mouth was a big fat wallet.

One of the pictures was quite a small one. Called *Smiler*. Most of the picture was this fist right up close, like it was comin out o'the paintin, with the thumb up in the air. Like Mr Bendy. Behind the fist was this mad smilin face.

Smiler was always sailin up an down the River of People. When he passed Mal he'd always make that sign, with his fist an thumb. Mal said it meant 'Grand', that the Thumbs Up sign meant somethin good was happenin. But what I saw was the fist, not the thumb. The fist that said, 'Don't ask me how I'm goin. Just don't ask.' Mal saw that too. *Law of Ssssh.*

'Street People. That's what my exhibition will be,' Mal says, 'but first we gotta go on the streets ourselves. Make some cash.'

He needs me. Mal needs me.

Just as we're about to walk out of the door, the phone rings. It's some fella askin if Mal wants to perform in the summer parade, the Big Summer Parade that happens every year. Half the city is in on it, an the other half watches it with all the visitors, an for that day all the streets are closed down in the centre of town an the whole place is full of colour an life an fireworks.

'What's the theme?' asks Mal, like he's not that interested.

Toys. The theme is toys. He agrees. We're both gonna be in the Carnival of Toys. Gas.

I'm held up by Mal's happiness, kept afloat an livin in the moment, by these things that are happenin to us. Maybe the tide is turnin, maybe things are goin to get better.

We're out on the street, an I'm dancin till mi little wooden feet are almost stumps. But mi heart, if I have one, is buzzin an trilling like a live thing. I'll just keep goin till I drop, cos that's what Mal wants.

La la la an the Kerry Dancin.

Mal is happy. I've never seen Mal so happy. Happy happy happy happy happy. Mal's Happy. I'm Happy. How are yer? I'm Grand. I'm Happy.

We're in one o'the oldy worldy streets cos the Invasion of the Hardhats is still goin strong in our normal spot. The River of People here's kinda slow like, full of vacant visitors floatin around.

There's a big fella with huge piercin eyes called Tony on the street. He's foreign, maybe Italian. Sound. He's an artist, draws people's portraits with crayons. Behind him, on a board, there's pictures o'famous people he's drawn at home, to show people he's good at makin likenesses. It's a dodgy job alright, paintin people's portraits, cos they wanna be flattered like. If they're ugly as an old boot, whaddya do? I mean, where does that leave yer?

'I could never draw portraits like him,' whispers Mal to me. 'That's not really art. Art is somethin' I do cos it's my callin'. This street performin', it's just somethin' to make money.'

Thanks a lot. That makes me feel really wanted. But I try an squash the feelin, cos I'm really happy. One or two things start going right for Mal, doesn't have to be much, an he talks like he's got paintings hung beside the Mona Lisa, know what I mean?

Anyways. Tony. He's sittin on the other side of the River of People. We'd just finished a run of the tape. We're takin a break. This yank with a big white beard an wearin a suede coat with lots o tassly bits comin from the shoulders, is givin Tony a lot of grief.

'I don't feel that's a very good likeness, do you my friend?' says the American in this *highanmighty* drawl.

'No?'

'I mean the whole shape of the face is completely wrong . . . And the eyes . . . do I have such mean, piggish eyes?' says the beardy fella.

What can you say when someone asks you that kinda question?

'Are you not happy with it?' asks Tony with this dodgy twinkle playin in his eye. 'Then you don't pay me.'

The tourist starts insultin him. Lookin at the other pictures on the board, sayin things like 'Is this supposed to be Frank Sinatra? It doesn't look anything like him . . . I really think you ought to get another kind of a job . . . I know something about art.' Know the kind o'way?

Tony's goin to hit him, for sure. He's not. He is. Instead he smiles. 'Maybe you're right. It isn't right. You know, sir, I would really like to try again, if you could spare the time?'

The fella sits again. The little stool almost gives up with the weight of him, an tis like the guy's doin Tony a giant favour. Tony looks real serious. Makin little careful marks. Lookin up like an owl, then down at the picture. The fella's sighin a bit.

'Just stay still for a minute longer, sir. It'll be worth it like . . . There. All finished.'

An there is the ugliest picture you ever saw. It's kind of a cross between a pig an a human. It has a huge snout dressed with a bushy white beard. Loads of spots. An the meanest eyes you ever saw.

'A perfect likeness,' says Tony, smilin. 'Whaddya think?'

The fella is shakin with rage. 'If we weren't on the streets I'd strike you down!'

'I did my best,' sighs Tony, eyes wide.

'You bastard!'

Tony stands up. He's very tall an the fella thinks twice. Then he roars at the yank. 'It's a perfect likeness man! It's a picture of your soul!'

A frozen moment where the fella tries to decide whether to take a swing at him anyways. Mal spots it, he's probably seen a lot of them kinda moments himself. He puts on the "Kerry Dances" really loud. The moment's broken, an the fella storms off down the street.

Mal goes 'Nice One, Tone!' an gives him the thumbs up an then it's back to the dancin.

Later that night, while Mal is paintin, he tells me the story of *Dorian Gray*. You know the one, about how Dor does all manner of horrors which never show in his face like, but only in the picture.

'Everyone changes, an' all yer deeds show in yer face,' he says, dabbin away. 'Except for you. You're lucky. I touch y'up now an again, an you'll last for ever.'

For ever. *I'll last for ever.*

Every day when Mal is in the jacks, I lap a little milk in a saucer. Creamy milk.

I was thinkin, maybe Mal won't want me anymore, if I turn into a real boy? I'm his puppet. His way of stayin alive. Here was his real love, the paintin. I knew that alright.

'I'm his real son.' said the photo of Joey.

But you're in fuckin England, an there's no way you're gonna come here you cute little shite says I, back to the photo.

'Mal?'

'Jesus,' sighs Rembrandt, 'Can you find somethin' quiet to amuse yerself, Lar? You're gonna have to realise I can't talk while I'm workin' . . . '

That's great. Fuckin great. I wear mi little apple feet to shavings an now I've gotta be floaty as a ghost, while Vincent Van Gogh creates the masterpieces. 'OK, Mal.' Why don't I tell the bollox to fuck off?

I start pretendin the bed is a cave, an I get right under it. I crawl past some crapped out old heater, then a *crinklecrinkleplastic* bag, that says "O'Beirn's Shoes For Fashion-Conscious Men." Mi little wooden body shakes with laughin as I think of Fashion-Conscious Mal. Which is mad like, cos it isn't that funny.

'Will yer shut up?' snaps Mal.

'*FASHION-CONSCIOUS MEN!*' I've lost it under there entirely.

I pull miself together. I look in the bag an there's a box. I open it. I stop laughin.

There's the spongy head of a woman starin up at me. It was a puppet. A puppet of an auldone. Pinky round face. Sharp dark button eyes, black dress an shawl. She was called Peggy O'Thatch an she looked mean an sweet at the same time. Her hair was like yellow straw, all done up in a bun, but with the wild bits stragglin down.

Mal said he couldn't get on with her. That's when he made me. 'I used some of the wood to make yer, an' the strings. Oh, an' the cross.'

Peggy O'Thatch has no arms. I have the arms of Peggy O'Thatch.

'She was a mean one alright. She'd love yer as long as you did what you were supposed to, worked hard, kept yer mouth shut an got Mass regular. But if you defied her, she'd never ever forgive yer . . . ' He went back to the paintin.

I walked up to Mal, whispered real close, 'Did . . . did she talk to you . . . like I do?'

Mal shook his head without lookin at me. Jesus, was I relieved. I looked at the lifeless head. I hated it.

What if she came back to life again, an started givin us lectures? Just as things had started to get good again?

I dragged the aul bitch back to her tomb under the bed. Back you go under there you, an be forgotten forever. With no arms she looked like the victim of some kinda massacre, she couldn't even cross herself hee hee . . . She was 'ARMless'! . . . hee hee.

Back into her fashion-conscious coffin.

Here's a dusty old photo album. How mad like, Mal sleeps on his yesterdays.

Windows into the past, Mal playin the Angel Gabriel in school play, Mal runnin race, face tight, stretchin his chest to the winnin string. Mal tall, respectable, clean cut, outside Fabric World, dressed in suit, holdin measuring tape an smilin, Mammy an Daddy makin a sandwich of him. 'This is mi first day . . . ' says Mal from the picture.

Daddy lookin like he had much better things for doing than

commemoratin his son's arrival at the shop, his hand to his chest, one finger pointin as if he'd just started makin the sign of the cross. An I look right into Mal's eyes like, an I cannot see a speck of his unhappiness. It's completely covered up.

An in we go, into the picture. A girleen with long hair is runnin up with the camera. It's Tara, before Mike, before her children. 'You'll have that moment for the rest of yer life!' she says to Mal with a look that says, 'don't do it man get out o'here,' beneath the smile. Which brings it home just how we change like, cos wasn't grownup Tara tellin Mal how he should have had the runnin of Fabric World, when we were at their house, an the drink was flowin?

She runs into the shop. There's a twelve-year-old carrot in front of her. That's their brother, Martin. Shows promise. There he is smilin like, an fingerin the great rolls o'fabric, all lollin around waitin for someone to buy 'em. When all else failed, Martin was to take over the shop for the auld ones, that was the plan sure enough. Foolproof. But he married a yank, an they wouldn't come back from San Francisco . . .

Mammy claps her hands. The whole shop stops what they're doin, except Daddy, who's ringin someone about an order.

'Malcolm's coming into work on a regular basis,' says Mammy.' Please do your best to make him feel at home. Show him the ropes. And I don't want to see any favouritism. He's to be treated just like everyone else, and I mean it.'

Sure, she meant it. Mammy was loved by all her cloth cutters. One Big Happy Family. But Mal was still favoured alright. The girls were doin the face down eyes up routine that Orla did. An what's this? Well one or two of 'em seem to be doin a bit more from what I can see . . .

'It's the Annual Stocktake. All hands on deck. There'll be overtime for everyone o'course.'

Daddy stands before them all like a General. Cos to him o'course the stocktake is of that order in a funny kinda way. It'd have to be, or wouldn't you die of boredom? An the dreary grind of loggin, checkin, an addin begins.

Mal an his mum are in a corner of the stock room.

'Does it suit you, Malcolm?'

'Grand.'

'You're a terrible liar . . . ' an she puts her little nail-polished hand on his arm. She can't bear to see him in pain, it looks like.

'I told yer. I wanna be an artist . . . something . . . '

'You've gotta provide for yourself Malcolm,' she says harder, an withdraws her hand.

Silence. Mal checks a list. Mammy sighs.

I turn the page of the album. Mal in front of Eros in Piccadilly Circus London, standin on one leg, tryin to be like the statue holdin a bottle instead of a bow. 'I've only been in London a couple o' weeks. I'm havin' a grand time! *I'M FREEEE!*' he shouts from the picture.

Another pose from the past. Jan an Mal sittin on a green slope on a very sunny day. Mal has a loose collarless shirt on an brown beads round his neck, a big belt an green corduroy trousers. He's very beardy, an needless to say there's a fag in one hand and, you guessed it, a bottle in the other. She looks like a fairy princess, her hair caught off her face, tumblin down her back, her eyes soothin, her smile slight like the Mona Lisa, secret an kinda regal. Her knees under the long skirt make a kinda platform for her to place her long royal hands on.

'Thank you. Thanks very much,' says Mal out of the picture, to a fella who was walkin an who took the picture for them. The fella gives them the camera. 'I'm not very good at taking pictures,' says the man with an outdoor smile an a little rucksack. 'Beautiful day for walking, isn't it? Goodbye.'

They watch the man walk down the hill into the valley.

'You could really believe this is where King Arthur lived, couldn't you?' moons Jan. The voice is gentle, clear as water.

'There he is now comin' out of that little clump o'trees, in his great silver armour, an behind him comes Guinevere, his beautiful but treacherous queen . . . ' an Mal kisses her ear an she moves her head like a cat. 'An' there's the handsome Lancelot who made her hungry with longin', an there's Gawain an Galahad an Bedivere, an all the Knights of the Round Table, an' there is Merlin the wisest man of all comin' up the rear . . . ' An she lies down an his eyes drown in hers, like he wants to dive into them, never come up again.

Very gently he loosens the ties on her shirt, an he sucks on her breast like a child.

She holds his head an stares up. The cloudy horses, warriors an faces unmoved by their love pass on by, across the blue. An it's one of those moments that's very short, an goes on forever.

'Mal. Mal. I . . . I have to . . . I'm going to have a child . . .'

Mal looks at her, confused.

How do you feel? Mal?

Sure I don't know.

They wait.

Jan, are you hundred per cent certain now?

I need to know how you feel . . . before I can decide anything.

What do you mean?

Don't be silly –

Jesus, I'm not . . .

Well if you weren't happy I'd consider all the options.

You mean abortion?

That's one of the options.

He looks at her. She looks at him. Her eyes say want me want us.

'Listen we don't have to be talkin about . . . don't don't . . . listen I'm fucking delighted! I'm delighted . . . '

He gives her a long kiss. They're both cryin.

An I'd be cryin too when I think of how it turned out. I mean they looked like they knew what they were doin. It all looked perfect.

I did cry. I gave birth to one tear. It scored mi cheek. I wiped it away quick. Slammed the book shut. Shoved it back under the bed.

Mal jumped up. 'Jesus Lar! Will you watch the telly or somethin',

God you're makin' me long for the days I could just shove you in the press an' forget about yer.'

I turned on the telly an perched on the armchair. There was a horror movie on about a kid's toy that was psychotic, an murdered any human it could get its hands on.

Mal got up an turned the sound down with a sigh.

'Wha?' says I.

'It's too loud. I'm tryin' to concentrate, alright?'

The toy stabs an aulfella with a scissor blade. Blood spurts over its little wooden face.

'I'd like to remind yer that you wouldn't have any fuckin' money for paints at all if it wasn't for me.'

'Who are you now, my mammy?' said Mal with a stupid smile.

'I'm only the one who makes the money around here o'course, so nobody listens to a fuckin' word I say.'

On the TV, some unsuspectin kid was looking at the toy an sayin 'Hey Pop, this is Really Cute! Can I take him home?' *Ha.* An I brood an simmer, lookin at the little toy murderer on the telly, an dream about leavin Mal, makin it on mi own, bein a film star . . .

Crash. In your dreams Lar. I'd never make the kind o'smash Pinocchio did in Mr Grimaldi's Theatre. Tis no great novelty anymore to see a Thing movin in films, or even in a play or show. They can make anythin look real.

But funny enough, when I dance in the streets an people know there's strings, an there's nothin to hide 'em, the crowd rubs 'em out with their own minds. We don't have to do anythin. In fact they like us more, cos they *can* see the strings. D'you understand what I'm sayin?

How could I survive without Mal?

The only people that would be interested in me like, I mean, the general public, would be freakshow journalists, who write edifying articles like 'I SMOTHERED THIRTY FELLAS IN MI LEFT BREAST'. Oh, an doctors. Doctors'd be well fascinated like. I'd be poked an x rayed an Christ knows what else. The religious nuts, Bornagains, they'd be another crowd clamourin for interviews, thinkin I was some kinda miracle. An o'course, criminals. 'Can you get through this air vent, an' open the door for us, Lar? Do it or we'll blow your arse off.'

If I told the world I was a Livin Thing, then I'd be prey to a crowd o'fools, an the only show business I could possibly get into at all'd be appearances on chat shows. Havin to cope with smart remarks like, 'Tell me Lar now, do yer ever knock on wood for luck? ha ha.' Roars from the studio audience, controlled as surely as if they all had the strings attached, an poor sad eejits, not havin a notion of it at all.

Fifteen minutes of fame an fortune, an then out on the shitheap, while them Doctors an Journos an Bornagains go off lookin for the next victim, an the rest of the world just points the finger at yer. I know this. I've seen it all on telly.

Back to me in the armchair. The film. Mal paintin.

'I'm going to kill you!' singsongs the Killer Doll to a small boy in the movie, who gurgles like it's the coolest thing in the world. I stick Joey's face onto the victim . . .

At the end of the film, the Killer Doll's burned down a house with a whole family inside it. But surprise surprise in the last minute some fuckin stupid deadbeat paddles around the smokey ashes collectin debris – 'What are you, little fellow?' – and there goes the psychotic toy into the deadbeat's pocket, ready for another Carnival of Death. An don't you just know that softeyed little fool is gonna be victim number one in the sequel?

When Mal had finished his paintin for the night he asked me what I thought. The warm feelin came up through mi feet an went right up mi body, into mi head.

It was a picture of us. Standin on a corner. I'm dancin, Mal is behind me. Mal is wearin a leprechaun hat like mine, smilin, stupid. It's not where we usually stand. Further up the street is a kid with a sign, lookin over at us, real sad, remindin me o'Tommy, that spacecadet from the Tribe we met. His eyes are kind of accusin us. Behind us is a shop with a big sign.CLOSING DOWN SALE. Watching us is one kid. Joey. Stab into the heart.

'I'm goin' to put the fella with the bucket in it too,' Mal said.

There's a fella in the street does a headstand in a bucket for what seems like hours on end. Mal says he's like the Hanged Man in the tarot pack, who's upside down, an sees everyone from a different angle like. Me too, I thought. Thank God I don't have to put mi head in a bucket just to see the world a bit different. Anyways, he can't see a fuckin thing except for the inside of a bucket, so he isn't like the Hanged Man at all.

'Whaddya think?' Jeez he really wants to know mi opinion.

'Why did you change everythin? When I'm dancin there's always a great crowd watchin us, an we don't work in that part o'the street, an I've never seen that kid there with the sign.'

'Things don't have to be exactly as they are . . . ' he says gently, considerin.

'Why don't they?'

'Cos Art's not like that.' An he starts explainin it all to me. How art is shaped an formed an in life things just happen.

Things just happen.

Things just happen like a wood boy comin to life; like gettin a terrible thirst on him; like he's turnin into a real boy.

An Mal's there in his bed. The little light is on, an he's sketchin in a book. I'm sittin on the bed too. An I want that moment to last forever.

I'm in heaven.

I'm gonna be a Thing forever. Tis not so bad being a Thing at all, you have a lot of freedom as a Thing, sure you do. An a *secretly conscious* Thing has a lot o'power, like the Killer Doll.

Next mornin, I started wonderin whether there were other things in this kinda twilight world of bein an not bein, like me. Maybe we could get together.

Mal asked me why I said 'how are yer' to the kettle. I asked a few more things, then I gave up. It seemed I was totally alone. Course the photographs *DO* talk to me like, but that's somethin different. Pyschic.

Most o'the time like, I had no time to think such thoughts,

lucky for me, I suppose. We were never in the house 'cept for the evenings, when Mal was paintin.

We're walkin up the tow path towards the workshop where the Parade's rehearsin. The sun is shinin – put that in yer diary – an we're walkin with this huge thin fella to this meetin to discuss the Big Parade. Mi head's pokin out the bag. Niall the Pole's got a tache, an the sorta mouth that if it stops movin settles into a kinda snarl. An lost eyes that look like he was happy once an had a soul inside but now it's flown away. Smart jacket, looks like he might be about to sell us an insurance policy. The whole town thinks he's God.

'Well, you see, the reason I brought the puppet along,' – starts Mal. Niall the Pole's mobile rings.

'Hi baby, howzitgoin'?' He's clearly not talkin to his mother. We stop walkin. Mal's lookin away, pissed off. An it dawns on me just then like what a great advantage it is to be tall. If you've to look up, you're always beggin somehow, an I should know.

While the Pole's makin love to his mobile, an Mal's lookin sour an crushed, the salmon fishers whisk their lines into the tumblin water. Two fellas in big rubber waders stand in the river that's runnin headlong to lose its small river identity in the vast sea, longin to be eaten by the ocean.

An the river reminds me of kids runnin out of school when the bell's gone. On the tow path, a boy an girl walk by, arm in arm.

'See yer tonight then baby,' growls the Pole an kisses the mobile like it's got baby's lips.

Pass me the sickbag. If I could throw up I would.

Mal's idea is this. He's gonna build a tower with a mechanism in it to go on a lorry. I'll be at the top an he'll be at the bottom. He'll be the puppet, an it will look as if I'm operatin him! Gas. The Pole thinks it's sound, but it has to go past the committee. Mal suggests a price for performin which is sad. Mal was never very good at sellin himself. But he does ask a fair price for makin the tower, which he insists on doin. O'course the price isn't fair at all like, cos there won't be any mechanism inside, an so the laugh's on us.

Suddenly, the Pole kinda turns himself off, looks out down the river, an says nothing. I can see Mal, who's known the Long One for a lifetime, doesn't know what to do with himself. The Pole goes an sits down on a bench.

'Come sit with me, Mal.' Mal follows him, a bit wary. The Pole can be a bit on the unpredictable side by all accounts. 'I was thinkin', last night. Remember the March of Fools an' Madmen?' His eyes went wet. Jesus, I thought, what have we done to deserve this? 'That was the First Parade. Remember the reaction like? Nobody'd ever seen anythin' like it before . . . Amazin'. It opened the hearts an' minds of the whole town. Everyone seemed to join in . . . '

'They did, they did so,' says Mal humbly, rememberin too.

'Everything's money, these days,' sighs Niall, touchin his goldy watch absentmindedly.

'Don't I know it?' says Mal, bitterly.

An Niall the Pole lets out a big sigh like he really meant it. 'Life's that cruel, Mal. It gives you, I dunno, a glimpse of possibilities, an' then it tears 'em away from yer . . .' Then, cheerin up a bit, an turnin to Mal as if *he* was the one holding them up, 'Come on now, we'd best be goin'.'

A fella in the river pulls up a salmon. A few on the tow path clap.

Night. The giant cranes feed on the town against a bloody sky. Mal's paintin. For the paintin he wears glasses. Little black-framed glasses that make him look a bit like Gepetto, if it wasn't for the scraggly beard, an long grey black hair tucked behind his ears. They make him look more like his granny to be honest with yer. He's sitting in the sheepskin coat, that looks like a pack o'dogs have been out worrying it. The whole room is lit with candles. He won't use the electric. He used the last pennies for the smallest tube of paint you've ever seen, an a bottle o'the brown stuff which was a wee bit bigger, but not much like – so much for his promise to not take drink before the exhibition. Ah well, it's a big improvement, I suppose. The dregs of his pocket bought him ten cigarettes.

Candlelight makes things live an dance. Things that have no life. Things that have no life.

Some bollox, well he wasn't a bollox at all like, more of a boffin I suppose, Mal was talkin to him in the pub once. The boffin gave him a lecture about molecules an how everythin was always vibratin like, but nobody could see it. In the candlelight, that's just how it looked.

The boffin also said there's this theory that Things are only there when you can see 'em, an when you can't see 'em, they vanish altogether. Isn't that completely cracked? I tried this out with the table once. I kept tryin to turn round quick to see if I could catch it appearin an disappearin an I couldn't. Bollox.

It was dark outside now. Only the yellow eyes of candles were left, makin the room look magic an holy. Flame's not livin like, not like an animal or a fella is livin, an yet it's kinda like tis more alive than an animal or fella could ever be. An if you tried to grab the flame . . . well it'd burn yer, it'd hurt terrible.

I took off the small woolly green jacket behind the bed, where Mal couldn't see me, an then undid the not so white shirt. I drew mi balsa wood hands in their white gloves over mi apple face, down over mi plywood body covered with foam, an stroked each limewood arm with the opposite hand, like I was a woman on telly havin a luxurious bath.

On mi right leather elbow joint I noticed a certain smoothness where the leather joined the wood, a blending. Then I felt the other elbow joint. It was the same. There was a smoothness on mi arms wasn't there before . . .

I was a Thing. A Thing. I couldn't be a kid ever, cos no kid in this world has ever been a Thing. They've been nothin, or they've been a kid. That's different. I don't want to be a kid. I don't want to shit an eat an piss an get spots an grow up an have girlfriends. *Get sick. Die.*

You're gonna die, right? Sure enough, one day. Probably in the most horrible pain you can think of, so horrible like you don't ever think it's gonna happen to yer until one day it does BANG.

98

A tear. *A tear*. Wipe it away quick.

Mal was away with the painting. He noticed nothing.

I should be happy. Look what happened to Pinocchio. He turned into a kid, an he an his daddy lived happy ever after. But life is not like fairy tales.

Mal found two coins that had gone in the armchair for a swim. He put them in the meter. On went the telly. Before you knew where you were another American cop was havin it away with some woman, an Mal's doin himself.

Jesus don't people ever get tired of this. An where did the magic candly atmosphere go to ? –

An as Mal's goin faster an faster an the cop's runnin through the streets again with the loud music an *bangbangbang*, the fella an his missus downstairs start goin ballistic. 'I'll do what I like, you cunt,' he says, an, 'Don't you fuckin' speak to me, prick have you got no respect,' she screams back, an suddenly I feel I'm in this madhouse.

'AAAIIIIEEEEE!'

An in mi dark heavy mahogany hips there's this terrible burnin pain. Real bad. I fall on the ground. An this great scream flies from mi mouth like a flock o'terrified birds. But Mal's makin out with the girl on the telly, so he hears nothin. Everythin goes black.

When I wake up, I'm in the bed. Mal must have thought I was sleepin, put me in the bed. Warm. It's still dark. Then I feel like I'm floatin face down in the water like . . . there's somethin damp underneath me.

I wet the bed.

I put mi hand down to mi britches an sure enough there's a wet patch, not a big one like, thanks be to god. But it's there alright. How could that . . .

I put mi hand to mi hips an slid it across. There's the smallest smallest bump.

A thing. Holy God, a thing.

I slide out of the bed, peelin back the duvet nice an slow an lookin at the little patch o'wet on the sheet. That'll dry so it will. Be dry before he wakes up.

I walked over to the blow heater. I turned it on. It was like a fuckin car startin up. I looked back. Mal stirred, but lucky for me he didn't wake up. I kneeled down before the fire. I felt the hot air hittin mi hips an dryin the wet flower on mi trousers. It melted away. Thankyou fire.

Let me just stay a puppet. God or world or whoever brought me into this fuckin shitehole to begin with. I don't wanna be a person it's too painful to be a person.

Mal wants me as a puppet. Can you understand that? Can yer?

Why can't things just stay the same? Why don't they last forever?

Cos they don't, Gobshite.

Art

Tis a fuckingood job I'm not scared of heights, I'm tellin yer. I'm on this truck, must be a small man's height above the ground, an then I'm on this tower, which is about another eight feet up. Course, I'm strapped in alright, cos Mal's had to make it look like there's some brilliant arrangement o'wheels an pullies in the tower itself, for which we've been paid a fortune.

O'course, the tower is just a box.

I saw Niall the Pole nosin about below, trying to get a peep inside to see how "the magic" (yours truly) was done. 'You're fuckin' amazin', Mal, you know that?' slimed Niall, puttin a long arm on Mal's shoulder. He gives him a sort o'manly hug, like there was more between 'em than there was like, an then looked up at me.

'You leave that fella alone, you gobshite!' I shouted down to the Pole, who's dressed by the by in a silver space suit an carryin a lazer gun. His moustache twitched like a furry caterpillar.

'Wha?' said the Pole, throwing Mal a *howthefuckdidyoudothat* look.

'The biggest pricks have the furthest to fall!' I said, as this kid dressed as a paintbrush whizzes past 'em on roller blades. Mal doesn't know where to look, an I'm laughin mi hat off. The Pole looks like a lost dog in a busy street. He wants to punch Mal, it

101

looks like. I'm sitting up there like an angel waitin to see what's gonna happen next. Mal raised his eyebrows mysteriously, pierced the Pole's eyes with his own, an shrugged his shoulders. 'See you after the parade,' he said, an then he smiled. The Pole smiled back uneasy. He walked off towards his army of silver-suited minions, as the laughin paintbrush on roller blades did wheelies around him. An you could see him convincin himself that he never heard me say them things at all, or he misheard them. We all prepare to march on the town, an the Pole, as big as he is, falls into the craic. As we all do.

I felt like God on the Parade, dispensing the Happiness from mi perch. An everybody was so happy, Well, they looked happy from where I was. Sure I thought, there's the answer to the world's sufferin that philosophers have spent their whole lives discussin. From where he is like, God cannot see that some people are havin an absolutely shite time of things. He thinks we're all havin a gas time, a party no less, cos when you're up high like, things do look very different. So when people pray about any number of disasters that are happenin to them, God, completely pissed off, says 'Will you just stop fuckin' wingein alright, an' enjoy the craic like?' See, he's having such a great fuckin time, an he thinks we are too.

I'm a philosopher. Is there no end to mi talents?

So they we were, like a Great Serpent of Life all coiled up in this carpark on the outskirts o'town, just waitin to attack.

An even the stonecloud, the shield of the sun, couldn't stop us. The heavens could open an we'd be goin anyway. Our Magic Snake of the Imagination all made up of the people of the city was gonna dance an sing an go mad in the streets, under the very feet of the metal bird monsters pickin away at the innards of the place, an shout out FUCK YOU FUCK YOU FUCK YOU . . . an give the grey little arteries of streets their yearly injection of colour an joy.

'Before we start on this year's parade, I'd like to thank you all,' said the toy soldier leading the Parade through the town. There was a long list of thankyous, an he was constantly gettin grief from this girl dressed as a rag doll standin next to him, but it was all an act I could see.

They were gettin us warmed up for our Invasion of the City. Our whole mad army buzzed with the anticipation of it all.

'LET THE PARADE BEGIN!'

Whistles. Hundreds of whistles. We're Comin. An Drums. Drums that are the heartbeat of our Great Beast. There is no city. We are the City. An We're Comin.

Everyone cheers, an we start to move off.

The toy soldier leads off with his army in the little green an yellow suits an they're makin one hell of a noise.

'Pete, look there's Donal at the back, now! Go for it, Donal!'

Marchin dancin, dancin through the streets. Crowds cheerin. Kids on Daddys' shoulders.

After the soldiers, what looks like a wooden train with two carriages of kids dressed as teddy bears follows 'em. The train's driven by a fella with a painted yellow face an all his clothes, they look just amazin. They're all different shades of brown an yellow. They look kinda grained. Just as if he was made of wood.

And today there is no River of People. We are the River of People.

After that, a gang o'kids all dressed in real old-fashioned gear, are spinnin hoops, an throwin balls, an skippin ropes an singin rhymes.

'Up an down the ladder
Turn your face together
Up an down the ladder
An Out Goes You.'

An as we turn down the oldy worldy streets, people throw streamers from windows, toast us with glasses, wave an shout.

Next comes a toy workshop with loads of elves, lookin like leprechauns, an kids on roller skates an skateboards an kids flyin kites, an sittin an bouncin on big rubber balls with faces painted on 'em –

Beep Beep!

– Two grown up fellas behind 'em sittin in giant pedal cars, an pretendin to be kids. Shoutin at each other. You crashed into me I did not!

Then there was this float like a giant book. Someone who was dressed as a kid, but was not a kid, opened the book, an all these characters came out of the book an then they went back inside. The kid closed the book an looked really happy, sayin somethin like 'I have been on a great adventure.' Sounds soft I know, but it wasn't at all.

We passed by one o'the hard-hat areas, which was all surrounded by the cage stuff. But today the surly beastmachines were still, an the men inside the cages had escaped. Ha Ha! Such is the Power of the Parade!

There was a float that was a box lorry, with the sides cut out of it, with lights inside. It was meant to be a computer screen. You could hear explosions an spooky sounds an some warrior woman was doin somersaults an fightin people, an her enemies were doin backflips.

Behind them came the Galactic Army, the Pole leadin the troops an firin water pistols at the crowd. Kids roarin.

Two rag dolls came down a high buildin on ropes.

Then there was us.

The World of Puppets, an I was the King. All the puppet operators, all of them, they were all below me like. I ruled 'em. As I looked down at everyone watchin me, faces like lights, I felt like I ruled the whole city. An I had Mal on a string. All around our float there were people with hand puppets an rod puppets talkin to the youngones in the crowd, who were havin to be held back by their mammies an daddies.

An so I could be the King of the Puppets better, Mal had made me a really big pointy crown. It was very heavy, but I looked great. I was so fuckin proud.

An I was laughin, cos it was great to be the one who was pullin the strings for a change, even though it only looked like it.

'Can't you dance better that that, Puppet?' I'd yell at Mal an Mal'd look all sorry for himself an appeal to the crowd an say, 'I'm doing my best!' an I'd say, 'Well it's not good enough, y'aul lump of wood! The children want to see yer dancin! Dance more, or on to the fire with yer. Dance more! . . . '

Dance more. Dance more dance more dance more –

I always wondered what people made of the last float of all.

Two grownups dressed as kids, a boy an a girl, sat on a truck an faced the cab. Fixed to the back of the cab, there was about thirty telly screens. On each telly was a different thing. The kids did nothing at all like. They watched the screens. Eyes wide.

There was a strange silence went over the crowd as they passed . . .

Then came a brass band an everyone smiled an cheered again..

How are yer? I'm grand.

Keep the aul smile goin

On the craic you will be flowin.

We was all in great form after, an there was mighty craic at the best party you can imagine, where the booze was flowin, an everyone wore masks.

I wasn't at the party like. Mal took me home which was fine by me, cos I could drink mi milk in peace, an consider the Great Day when I saw the town from above, all pumped up with Life. Mal said that some bastards was sayin this parade was not as good as last year, but I was in it like, an I can officially report it was the best ever.

There was a film on the telly kinda washin over me. About Van Gogh, poor bastard. No one gave much of a fuck about him or his paintins. Even when the sad bastard cut his ear off no one paid any heed to him like. No wonder he topped himself. An now his fuckin paintins are worth millions. I wondered whether anyone'd give him any heed if was alive now, an tryin to get 'em in a gallery. Not a chance. An what sick luck, don't you think, to be a genius an die in poverty an misery while all these rich bastards make a fortune out of yer? An all yer life waitin for a few bolloxes just to say, 'That's good Vinny. Fair play to yer. Paint a few more.' That's gonna be Mal, I'm thinkin. I brushed the thought off me. *Law of Ssssh*. An I'm thinkin, aren't you better off to make a kid smile, than reach for the stars?

Uuuuhhhhh.

I hear a kinda groan in the room. Shit. Relax. It's just the poor woman below us wakin up from a punch or somethin.

Groan.

Jesus. I turn mi head slightly towards the bed. There's something movin under the bed. I know what it is . . . no.

'Feck yer, yer little applehead. Gimme mi arms back!'

Peggy O'Thatch. Her crowy squeak. She squirms out from the bedcave an stands unsteady, in her little black dress an shawl, her straw hair hangin round her face, draggin her strings an her little wooden cross. The telly makes strange patterns on her ghosty hair an face.

'Who the feck do you be thinking y'are, you little bollix.' Then suddenly she bends her head quick. 'Say a decade for swearing now, Peggy O'Thatch . . . ' She falls to her knees with a thud. 'Gimme mi arms back!' she shrieks.

I was scared shitless.

'How can I pray to Our Lord without hands to clasp? How can I scrub an' clean without mi arms?'

Then suddenly, It's up with the legs, an she's dancin! Starts to sing.

'*Diddlyeyedie, diddlyeye,*
Diddlyeyedie, diddlyeye,'

'I can still dance well enough! Don't need arms for dancin'!'

She's very close to me know like. She stops singin. She throws herself on the ground, grabs mi legs with her legs an pulls me off the chair an on to the floor, screamin 'Gimme mi arms back! They're mine!'

I tear miself away. 'They are *my* arms now, so they are,' I yell back, 'And they're turnin into flesh if you want to know . . . '

She cackles an cackles, like she'd be sick if she could.

'You're a big fool. You're just a puppet. Puppets don't turn into Breathers. That's just in stories. An hear me now! If the whole of the rest of your body turns to flesh an blood, them arms will still be *my* arms. They'll still be made of wood, an they'll still be wantin' to clasp together an' pray, an' scrub the stone steps.'

She lies sprawled across one of Mal's paintins, the one of him an me an the kid watchin us, like she's a woman in a film, lying on a big bed . . .

'Get real Lar! Get a life,' says Joey all of a sudden, from the picture of Kensington Gardens.

Peggy O'Thatch rolls around over the paintin, pissin herself laughin. I open mi mouth to say somethin about the paintin an then I gasp like.

Joey is standing there. In the room. Grown up. Holding a bag.

'I'm coming.' he says.

An I'm screamin an screamin. I get up, to take a run at Joey, an Peggy O'Thatch grabs me, an we're fightin, On the telly some old film's started, an this fella Elvis is singin, 'Cos I don't have a wooden heart.'

Suddenly her body goes limp an dead in mi arms. I've killed her. Great. I can't believe it. I drag her back to the box an put her inside it. I tape the box up good an tight. Just as I'm thinkin I dreamed the whole thing, 'Someday this is where you're gonna be, yer little bollix, in a box, an I'll be openin' it up, so I will, an yankin' the arm from yer socket . . . '

I watch the box for a good while. Nothing happens. I cry. Another tear.

Joey's gone.

The key's chattin with the lock. The door opens. Mal falls in. Downstairs they'll be thinkin a bomb's been dropped.

'Made it,' he mumbles.

Made it to shore, this time.

Unconscious.

He made it alright. We made it, I should say. To the Not So Great Exhibition.

Buzz buzz buzz. Framin an lightin, an all that craic.

O'course by this time Mal was already gettin disillusioned.

Inside. An the more he did, the harder he worked an the happier he pretended to be. I mean, I knew it was gonna happen right from the start like. He set himself up for the disappointment. But then, when you've got nothin to hope for, you'll make the most sad little option into a dazzlin opportunity. If you're a failure, that kind o'trick keeps you in good form. An that's what Mal was, I guess.

He acted at first as if every art critic in the land was gonna be at The Belly of The Whale, café/restaurant/wine bar/art gallery – notice like that "art gallery" is last on the list. Some fella from the local paper was one o'the most influential guests that first day. He did a whirlwind tour round the pictures an spent the rest o' the time chattin away, stuffin as many vol au vents an free glasses o'wine as he could down his neck. He came in with a tall fat fella from one of the other galleries in town, who sipped *Ballygowan* an stared down his nose at the pictures. His lips were tight an pursed like he smelled somethin bad, an he bent his knees to look at the paintins, as if he was thinkin of having a shit right in front of 'em.

An swoopin round the place, with the "finger buffet" was Pandora, the café owner, in a flowy dress. She was kinda sexy I suppose. English. Posh. Ought to be on a horse or wearin skis. Mal tried it on with her, not that that's sayin much like. If it has breasts, he's off.

She was obviously tryin to attract an arty upmarket crowd. Not the kinda clientele that'd go in SHTUM you know, who'd be yer average busker like, but yer trendy wives an the kinda people that go for drama lessons. She wanted that crowd in, cos that was the sort o'crowd she wanted to belong to herself.

In all fairness like, well, she was a pretentious cow. Mal realised it in the end. Funny like, cos normally he'd be the first to spot that kinda shite, but cos he wanted to get into her knickers he missed it completely, until she told him that she only wanted a business relationship, an then the fog lifted an he saw her exactly for what she was –

'That bitch knows absolutely fuck all about art!'

– But she was forever holdin forth like, with her small cigar stuck in her fingers, as if she'd done several degrees in it. She was takin a decent percentage too if he sold anythin, which we both thought was a fuckin cheek, as it was Mal that got some o'the classy punters Pandora was cravin into the place to begin with.

'Very interesting, Mal,' says Volovon between mouthfuls, suckin a mushroom off his fat little finger..

'Hmmmmmm.' considered Springwater.

'Real Vitality, real Earthiness . . . '

Get the picture? Ha ha.

Volovon's eyes were the eyes of an even bigger failure than Mal, as he stared into the paintings. As he thought about all the paintings he'd never painted.

When you think about it like, it must be really terrible goin to see an exhibition if you've always wanted to paint an never done it, or a play like, an always wanted to act an never been on a stage. Terrible. Terrible. That's why I suppose, it's better to be Mal than Volovon. In a way.

In a way it is.

Springwater's missus bought the one of me, Mal, Joey, the lad with the sign, an The fella with his head in a bucket.

'I'm sorry to see that go,' says Mal, an Missus Springwater jerks her head at him, like a gull on the lookout for food, as if to say 'Keep it then. I'm only buying it for your sake,' an Mal bows his head to the floor, like he was her butler or somethin.

Some sad masochist bought the one of Philip the Deadbeat an his dog. Mal told the story of how he'd been killed in a knife fight in Dublin, though o'course I knew better, that we'd put the curse on him. 'If there's a story to go with the paintin' you can add money on it,' said Mal to me up in our place once. He's right there. See, then the O'Trendies are buyin the story as well. An a story makes it even easier to talk about with guests as you throw the wine down yer neck an suck on yer sushi.

I hate those fuckin people. Livin off the artists' sufferin. Never takin the risks. Buyin the fuckin myth, like that opera, what is it, *La Bohême*, where everybody's havin a gas time burnin their masterpieces to keep warm but what the fuck, let's go an get wrecked anyway. Then the curtain comes down anyways, an sure no one's really dead at all.

Jeez Lar, yer starting to sound a bitter man yerself.

In the pub after the openin. A cheque is in the bank. The Great Ship Exhibition is startin to take on water already, an the wind has dropped. Mal tries to keep the thing afloat by takin on Porter, an for a short while it appears to be workin. He's still on course. A few friends around him like, a few *welldonegodIjustdon't-understandhowyerworkisnotmorerecogniseds*, a few drinks bought. But one by one, them friends decide the life raft is a better option, an they float out into the open street. Brendan who got him the exhibition, is the last man to jump the ship . . .

'You're a good friend to me, Brendan,' slurs Mal, 'but you know I've had it with the paintin' . . . What's the point of humiliatin' yerself before people, Brendan?'

'People love your paintings. What are you talkin' about?' says Brendan wearily. Mal looks down, smiles to himself for a second, then the smile melts, and he stares into Brendan's eyes. 'There was a couple of paintings bought now,' says Brendan, waggin the finger in his head. 'Let's look on the bright side for fuck's sake,' he's thinkin.

'I know, sure I know, an I'm very grateful to you an all that . . .'

'Now, I didn't say it for – '

'You didn't, you didn't, sure you didn't . . . I know *that* you bollox sure don't I know *that* . . . you're a good friend to me . . .'

One of the things I hate about people when they've drink taken is how they fuckin repeat everythin a million times, as if they just thought of it, an expect you to pretend you've never fuckin heard it before.

Brendan says goodnight, sayin somethin about Mal getting another exhibition in his gallery, an how this time he won't be treated like crap by any fancy agents. He puts a friendly hand on Mal's shoulder an says somethin like 'it's been a grand day for you Mal . . . I'm certain it'll be the start of somethin',' an Mal's face twists like it was an aul dishcloth bein wrung out. Cos Mal knows o'course, or *thinks* he knows, that the Not So Great Exhibition is goin to lead to a few bills being paid, an a night or two in the pub, an that's it. Lucky for Mal, Brendan doesn't see all this facetwistin, an goes away to put his own head down an go back to his wife an his warm house.

'Just you an me now Lar, just you an me . . . ' Mal looks down a glass tunnel.

There's one or two o'the regulars lookin at Mal now, an knowin exactly the way things'll be goin. He'll start off with the 'I'm grand' routine, huggin an kissin as many as'll let him get his arms around 'em. Then he'll pull me out o'the bag, an we'll do a song an dance routine on the bar. Then he'll go all quiet like for a bit an either start actin like a cornered dog or he'll start abusin people, imaginin they've been slaggin him like, which if they *have* been is usually cos tis either the drink talkin from his mouth or theirs.

Usually Mal storms out then, sayin somethin like – 'I'm never stepping into that fuckin' place again!' and – '*JussbecosIstarttakinthepissoutothemtwofellaswiththemobilesstupidbastardstheyfuckinshouldnallowmobilephonesinthatpubin* ANYPUBALRITE?
ALRITE?'

And here we are on the street, just as I said we would be.

Standin in the rain. From every pub the laughter an the craic foams outa doors an windows. Doors guarded by bouncers. The whole city's laughin except for us.

In a doorway. Mal lights a cigarette. A big drip kisses the tip an it hisses an goes out.

'Fuckin'shite. Muss have a light somewhere . . . '

Across the street a young lad, one hand proppin himself up against the wall, throws up on the pavement under the orangey light an I'm thinkin God is this what I was brought into the world for, what does it all mean an all that crap you always think in these kind of moments.

Suddenly Mal starts laughin. Laughin until he can hardly stand.

'THIS PLACE . . . THIS PLACE IS SHITE!' he screams . . . Then he goes quiet.

'Mal, are you ok?'

Silence, then he turns to me sittin in the bag, with a fakeyserious face on him.

'I've just been havin' a little talk with Mr Bendy, an he has recommended that we are in need of a pick-me-up, a little vacation to take away the blues.' Mal puts on this fruity English voice an waggles his thumb around.

'Is that right? Where we goin'?' says I to Mr Bendy.

'It's a mystery, my boy,' says Mr Bendy.

An me, Mal, an Mr Bendy go off on our next adventure.

Holey

Scott had been drivin for Spelmans for three months, an in that time he'd crashed the small van, the large van an the bosses car when he was takin it over for a wash. You'd have thought that Mr Spelman would have taken this for a sign o'somethin, maybe that Scott couldn't drive like, but Scott's job was a return favour to his mammy. I suppose Mr Spelman thought his whole fleet of cars could end up in the junk yard in return for the favours of Mrs O'Mara.

Scott, just eighteen, was named after Scott in *Neighbours*, so his mammy said. There's no Scott in *Neighbours* now. He's long gone. An Scott O'Mara was named after the first Scott who was a dark-haired fella an vanished into oblivion, not the second Scott who was blonde an got real famous. Despite the fact that they looked nothin at all like each other, said Scott O'Mara, these two lads were playin the same person, when anybody with the smallest pinhead o'sight would have seen they were completely different. An no one said to Scotty number two – not even his granny or his daddy – 'Howzitgoin' Scott? You're looking a bit different this mornin. Been to the hairdressers to have a blond rinse?' or anythin.

But the strange thing was, said our Scott, that after the second Scott had been in the story for a few weeks, you completely forgot there'd ever been another fella actin the part! That's what his mum had told him anyhow.

What would happen I thought, as we were speedin along at 90 mph an I was tryin to think about somethin else, if this happened in the real world. Let's say you went into a shop every day for a paper. An every day, you had the craic with the woman that sold it to yer. She was glamourous an good lookin in her 30s. An one day you went into the shop an lo an behold she was dumpy as a grandma. Then when you made some kind of an enquiry about the woman you knew, Grandma told you she *WAS* the woman you knew, an everyone else who came into the shop talked to her as if nothin had happened, just like Scotty in *Neighbours*? What would you do, like?

His aunty Betty told Scott O'Mara that there was no way he was named after either o'the Scotts in *Neighbours*, cos *Neighbours* hadn't even started when Scott was born like.

Anyways I'm ramblin. Pressin the fastforward button we ended up in some kinda trad session in a little farmhouse with auld fellas playin twenty fives an loads o'jolly talk about death, sellin sites, an the price o'cattle, laced with a few dregs o'poteen.

A leathery auld one took us back into town. Flat cap. Hands washed in soil. All I can remember about the journey like, as we chugged along the lane was the temperature gauge for the engine in his car was about the size of a kitchen clock.

'Pinched that from a vat in a creamery,' he laughed. 'Works a treat . . . '

Then a mobile rang.

'Fuck fuck fuck,' he mutters. 'Press that blue button for me, will yer, Mally?'

'I'm waiting on yer Padraic,' says a voice with a poker up her arse.

'I know y'are. I know . . . I'm on my way . . . '

The fella motioned Mal to press the blue button again. 'Twas

Herself. The Voice of Doom.' He laughs for a second, then it turns into a fierce coughin. The car slows an swerves.

Fuck, we're gonna crash!

Jesus Christ he's gonna die, an we'll be blamed cos we're strangers, an end up buried in some field, but the cough turns back into a laugh again, as if it just came up to remind the fella to make the most o' things cos he hadn't long to go like.

'Great yokes, them mobiles,' says the farmer.

'Brain tumours,' mumbles Mal.

'Means you can always be reached . . . '

'Reached?' scoffed Mal.

'O'course, sometimes it's better not to be reached,' he laughs, like he an Mal shared some great understandin about the difficulty of women, an the car swerves again as the fella's little joke brings on another fit o'coughin.

We made it into town.

'Watch out for the guards now . . . they're fierce down on the drink these days . . . new sergeant . . . bollox . . . drop you here will I?'

There was as good as anywhere like. I suppose anywhere in the Middle o'Nowhere will do just fine. Two streets of old houses, an a fair few new ones fattenin the town. A supermarket. A church. All bathin in the sick orange light. An not a soul to be seen.

'Jeez, don't you feel just like you're in a film?' says Mal.

'No,' said God cos he pissed on us. He must have been fuckin burstin to go. I put mi head back an let the drops go into mi mouth.

We ran across to the church. Even in the orangey light, it looked very well; neat flower beds; well cropped lawn. 'This town's makin' sure they have the full access to Paradise,' quipped Mal. He crossed himself. He must have really been out of it. His daddy always crossed himself when he passed a church. His mammy did it too to please his daddy, an the kids did it cos they'd get a bollockin if they didn't.

The church door was open. Great. There was a few fake candly lights on. The drink gave Mal the knockout punch an he was gone.

Black.

I woke up. It was still night outside. Mal was snorin away. I clambered out o'the bag an looked around. I was dyin o'thirst. Then I remembered there was water at the door, where Mal dipped his fingers in.

Click clickety click. I walked over to the door where we came in. I couldn't reach the little sink set in the wall, so I pulled a kinda prayer chair up to it. Still I couldn't reach, so I put a few books on top of it, an climbed up.

'Who are you? What are you doing here?'

Swish! This reddy curtain goes across. Standing there, framed in a wooden box, is this fella with white cropped hair an wearin a dog collar. Then he starts speakin some funny language which I take to be the Latin that I've heard Mal talk about.

For some reason this kinda makes me laugh an the priest turns the volume up. I laugh more an more till it gets uncontrollable. Crash I go onto the stone floor, an serve the bollox right I hear you say, an you'd be right I suppose, at this stage.

Urrrrrrrrrrrrrrr. That's Mal wakin up.

'So the Devil has come to the parish at last?' whispers the priest, just as if he's in one o'them films where kids get possessed. He's shittin himself an tryin to pretend he isn't, which is pullin him to bits inside. Mal raises his head from the bench he's lyin on.

'I can make mi head spin right round, if you wanna see it,' says I, tryin to lighten the tone.

'Shut up, Lar, don't frighten the poor man,' says Mal.

It's clear after a bit that the priest, Father O'Leary, is havin a bit of a nervous breakdown. I mean, he'd been spyin on us from that box since we came in like. He probably lived in that box. That is not the action of a well man. Anyways we calm him down, an tell him the whole story, well not the whole story, but a fair bit of it . . . Now come on, who would tell the whole story? There were some bits he would not want to be hearin.

'I suppose it's a kind of a miracle,' an he smiles, 'You've found your way into my church . . . ' It was kinda pathetic. I let him stroke mi *applemaybeturningintoskin* face.

He tells us the story. He's new to the parish. The recent priest was very popular, an could say mass in twenty minutes flat, but died one day with a heart attack right there on the altar tryin to break a new record. When O'Leary came he was not a popular man, because Mass got longer an longer an was now runnin at 42 minutes.

He'd got some hate mail in the post. Made up from bits o'newspaper. It said things like – "Speed up or else!" an an even more threatenin one which said – "Snails are pests and can be eliminated."

He went to the gardai like, but didn't want it advertised that somebody was puttin this pressure on him, so they couldn't do much an found out absolutely fuck all.

The letters were still comin, an he was losin the run of himself.

Suddenly his face lights up. Basically the idea was that I was gonna be dressed up as an angel. Or even Jesus himself on the cross. Like I was a new statue an then in the middle o'Mass on Sunday, which was the next day, I was gonna start talkin to the congregation.

This was a gas idea alright. It'd put the fear o'God into the local people. They'd start comin back to Mass, do what O'Leary wanted, an the hate letters would stop. Mal wasn't sure that he wanted people back to Mass, that they were better off out of it altogether, but I could see he couldn't say that to O'Leary. The whole thing still cast its spell over him. Like he really wanted to believe it but he couldn't any more.

I wasn't happy with the idea of going on a crucifix, mainly cos I was scared that Mal might notice somethin, about how I was changin like. They didn't think that I could pull the Virgin Mary off. So it was decided that I'd be a statue of the Angel Gabriel in flowy robes.

Before Mass starts, Father O'Leary makes some announcement

about the new statue, saying it arrived yesterday evenin. He blesses me. Sighs from the crowd. More time taken.

Cough cough murmur murmur all the fellas standin at the back like they don't belong in church at all . . . one or two youngones pointin an smilin at the new statue, me.

Tut tut tut. People looking at watches. Big sighing. I even heard some enormous woman saying at the front, "Come on, will yer father, cos I've got to get the dinner on." Anyways, just as O'Leary's about to give the final blessin an some of 'em have already set off to be the first away so they don't get caught in a traffic jam, I cry out –

'WHY ARE YOU ALL IN SUCH A HURRY? DO YOU NOT REALISE THAT GOD CREATED YOU?'

It was like a freezeframe on the telly. Gas. Total gas.

'IS AN HOUR SO VERY MUCH TO GIVE HIM ONCE A WEEK?'

Hee hee. There was this stunned silence. Some sat down. Some tumbled to their knees. One or two o'the auld ones started to cry an set the mumble train goin, that was their prayers.

'THIS IS NO TIME FOR PRAYERS,' I says, 'SHUT YOUR MOUTHS an LISTEN TO THE MESSENGER FROM GOD.'

Mumble train comes to a halt. Others sit. Some o'the fellas come in from the back. Murmurin from ripple of lips miracle Jesus it's a miracle.

I can't remember what I said like after that, just stuff about bein kind an lovin yer neighbour an money wasn't all it was cracked up to be. They were all dead emotional like, but I wondered in the end whether it would make any difference at all.

I saw a good few of 'em go up to O'Leary, shakin his hand, an one fella said, 'I'm sorry, Father.'

I had people prayin to me the whole day. The woman who not long ago had been moanin on about her dinner had whizzed out the rosary beads. It was weird. If we'd sold tickets we'd have made a fortune.

I was gettin a bit bored like with all this adulation, an just for somethin to do like I closed mi hands in prayer an put mi head down. They all gasped together. A little lad at the front said. 'Excuse me angel –'

'Timmy, will you come back this minute!' But the kid ignored her.

'Will there be room for everybody in Heaven? Are people of all different colours there?'

''Tis gorgeous in Heaven sure. All of us bathed in God's Love,' says I, in the holiest voice I can manage.

Timmy's Mammy an one or two o'the others start to cry, as at that very second a blade of light comes through the window onto the kid. Even the scrubbed fellas at the back are lookin moved . . . A fat fella falls to his knees. 'Forgive me for doubtin' yer. Please forgive me.' More tears. I feel like blabbin miself like. I feel like that cos they believe me. Cos it took hardly anythin to make them believe me.

A couple of angels in black coats, hopin very soon to trade them in for white flowy robes an join the Heavenly Choir, wanted to say the rosary at mi feet all night, but O'Leary said they should be goin to their beds. Which was grand, cos then they could get me out of the robes.

Mi arms were smoother now. Mi chest was startin to feel softer too like. Mal was talkin to O'Leary an he didn't see. The trousers were a bit dampy. I told Mal I'd fallen an there must have been some water on the floor.

'You look as if you pissed yerself,' he said, smilin.

I laughed.

O'Leary looked a happy man when he dropped us off into the next town. But Mal said after he'd gone, 'Ah, they were on their knees alright today. By Tuesday they'll be sayin' it was all a trick.'

An with that sad thought we got into a big purple ambulance with a woman who wasn't much smaller than what she was drivin, who talked about Energies, Laylines an Reincarnation, an told us the People of Israel came from Connemara.

Son

'I'm coming,' said Joey from the photograph, as Mal slammed the door.

Wink wink message machine. 'I've got a secret,' it says.

'Jesus, Mal, put the fire on first now, will yer?'

'And when did you start feeling the cold?' Mal meant nothin by this o'course, but it was like he stabbed me in the –

Beep.

Hello Mal. This is David speaking. David from England. Joey's . . . stepfather. I wonder if you could call me when you get home. Please.

Beep.

Sorry Mal. This is David again. Sorry

Jan's dead. Jan is dead. What Breathers call the Big C.

Mal, still in his aul coat, perches on the edge of the red chair like a gnome, with a fag. He knew somethin was up before he'd phoned back. You could tell like, the way David was tryin to be normal. The room was still snubbin us with the cold. Mal shivered.

Then his body's still. He's wrestlin with the pain of it inside like, not just the pain of Jan dyin, but like a whole chunk of his life has been cut out of him.

He's imaginin Jan's belly covered with blisters like rottin blackberries, the belly he stroked, an the warm red lips, dry an pale.

Suck on the fag. Stab yer lungs. That's it Mal. That's life. Being human. Jesus isn't life grand? An for a minute there I'm enjoyin the fact that it hurts him, for all the times he's hurt *me* . . .

But then I wanna say something. Something nice an soft. My pain is his pain.

Jeez what I wouldn't do to have mi own pain an tell him to fuck off like an deal with his own. *I do.* I *do* have mi own pain. So what the fuck do I want his for, as well?

David said he would have had Mal at the funeral, but Jan didn't want it. She thought Joey was havin to go through enough, without havin Mal there as well.

'Daddy!' yelled the photo.

'Shut the fuck up!' I shouted at the picture.

Mal shot a *losttheplot* look at me. A questioning look. An, "Are You Really There?" look. Glassy jewels in a puffy face. Then he looks down, then away. He lights another cigarette.

'Mal?'

'Fuck off.'

I'm scared. Don't be mad, Lar. He's just stunned, that's it like. Just can't take it. Doesn't want to talk. Wouldn't talk to anyone. Not even Joey if he was in the room.

I climb onto the bed an look at him. Can't take mi eyes off him. Don't know why. Glued to his grief like. An I can hear kids slaggin each other in the street, an the telly in the flat below us, an tired steps chuggin up the stairs in the corridor an a stranger's door closin. Mal's thoughts tumble around these sounds an through mi head.

An I understand a thing I didn't know before. That it wasn't like what I saw in the photo, when Jan told him she was pregnant. She'd got pregnant cos it was his last chance to prove himself to her. That he could be reliable an solid an dependable an all the things she thought she wanted him to be. When he didn't get his act together when Joey came into the world, she got rid of Mal an found herself another man.

How many kids come into the world cos of the pain of their

mum an dad, just like me with Mal, just like Joey with Jan? Wouldn't it be better to be dead than carry all your parents' pain about with yer?

Mal looked up at me. I knew somethin bad was gonna happen then.

He came over to the bed an picked me up, then he threw me against the opposite wall. He rushed over an I thought he was gonna crush me with his foot. I rolled over quick but then he leaned over, grabbed me, opened the press, threw me in, an slammed the door.

'Mal. Will you let me out Mal . . . ' I said, all tearful.

He ignored me. Turned on the telly.

'Mal, what have I done?'

'Mal?'

'Will you shut the fuck up!' he shouts back at me. 'You can't really talk at all. It's just me. You're just a fuckin' voice in my head.'

I thought for a minute there o'sayin somethin smart like, "If I'm not really talkin, then why are you speakin to me?" but I thought, better keep the gob shut. An anyways I was too upset. I was cryin.

Jesus, I was cryin. Mal's gonna see me cryin. What'll happen now? What could happen? If I told him I was turnin into a boy, he wouldn't believe me. Maybe he'd kill me.

If I *was* alive. *Really* alive. He might kill me if I was alive. Anyways he certainly wouldn't be sendin me skippin off to school with mi sanbos an school books, like Gepetto did in the movie. *I have to think! Think!* Maybe I ought to just play the Thing for a bit, till he gets over this sadness. Wasn't he grand until he heard the news?

I bet it's hard for Breathers to feel sorry for me at this stage. I mean, amn't I only a piece of wood? Well there was no fuckin helpline for *me* to phone. There was no one to go to. No one. He made me. He could do what he wanted.

I was havin a small piss in a bucket when the phone rang.

It was David. Then it was Joey. They were comin over in a

week. Joey wanted to come. Jesus Christ my world was cavin in.

Mal puts the phone down.

'Do you hear that?' he says all fierce. 'My son is gonna come to visit me . . . ' Then he walks across the floor an slams the door. I hear his feet tappin the stone steps in the corridor.

Inside me, I let go like. Tis a terrible thing when you're waitin for someone you love to go out so you can relax an be really yourself. Yourself.

I started thinkin again. I mean like, what am I like? Puppet or boy? I'm not a real boy. I can never be a real boy. Can I? Can I be a real boy? I'm a wooden puppet made to look like a middle-aged fairy fella from a time long gone. A kind of a fella that never really even existed except in the minds o'film producers an tourist guides . . .

Fiddle de Dee an Diddly Eye

Fiddle de Dee

The jigs an the reels

Fiddle de Dee

An bodhran

How I hate 'em. The punters, thinkin, believin that that's me.

'It isn't ME you herd of bolloxes. THAT ISN'T ME!!!' I yell from the press into the empty room.

Mi chest is heavin a bit. An I'm thinkin, Jesus don't tell him, don't tell him now . . . How's he gonna miss it you wooden fool? Yer chest is startin to move. You're actually startin to breathe!

I could hear Peggy O'Thatch tryin to escape from her shoebox under the bed, wrigglin, scratchin an moanin, mumblin prayers. After a while, she gave it up.

Mal came back a few hours later. Fear shot up mi back.

I'd got out o'the press. I was sittin on the chair watchin the telly. A couple of people were makin it up. They were both cryin. Their faces were squeezed like dishcloths.

No such scenes for me an yourman.

I slink off the chair like some beast used to being beaten. Mal staggers to the chair an drops into it. He sits there, like he's sucked in by the box an watches the film. Before you know where y'are, the TV couple's in bed an Mal has his thing out again. Jesus, Am I mad.

'What are you doin' there exactly?' says I, takin the tone of Peggy O'Thatch. Course, I know somethin of what he's doin, but I wanna ask like, to shame him. If I say nothin he can go on treatin me just like a Thing . . . But he didn't answer, just carried on doin it till it was over.

I have a thing comin an then I'll be doin it too.

Jeez, if only the Great Boy God Joey could see his daddy now, sweatin an wet after a night on the tear, wankin over an illusion.

These two on the film are most likely dead at this stage. Tis an old film. You're wankin off with the Dead.

Sick sick sick.

Next day, over his woodshavings, he apologises. I can't believe it. The weather's fine an he wants to go out an make some money. I'm so keen like, so keen to get back into the fucker's good books that I say ok grand, cos somehow, an I don't know why this is like, I feel as if the whole thing is my fault.

While he's away takin a piss, I'm drinkin the milk as usual an then I pick up the pack o' woodshavings to take it back to the shelf. Suddenly, I feel this kinda churnin like somebody's just scooped a space out inside o'me with a spoon an I have a terrible terrible hunger. *I'm hungry.* I open the packet, take one o'the woodshavings in mi mouth, an chew it a bit. Then down it goes . . .

I scream mi fuckin head off, cos it suddenly feels in mi neck like somebody's put a light to me.

Mal doesn't hear me.

Out on the streets, dodgin the hardhats an their beastmachines, are flamethrowers swallowin flame, jugglers, movin statues, as well as the usual crowd o'muzos, an a few kids doin street theatre. It's like everyone suddenly realises that the summer's nearly over, an they've gotta make a fortune, cos there's not much longer to go. Like beasts with an instinct.

The hardhats had moved on from our regular spot so we went back to it.

'Jesus.'

Where the buildin society had been, where Fabric World had been, there was a big hole. Like the street was a smile with a tooth missin. Mal just stood there. Stood there.

Stood there.

People flowed around an past, but Mal just stood there. Cos even though he hated the fuckin shop an everythin it stood for, it still kinda belonged to him. But now it was gone. Completely gone. Like someone had said, "I don't give a fuck for your feelings or your memories."

We started the dancin. An as another tenner fluttered down into the bag, Mal whispered to me, sad an low, 'I dunno, Lar, maybe we should go to America.'

An I thought, Yes. You're on. Let's go. Now. On the next train. On the next plane. Let's cut all the strings an get away together. You an me. Lar an Mal. Let's go. Don't wait for Joey, Mal. He's only gonna make you feel like throwin yerself in the river. Sure, he's yer flesh an blood, but he hasn't grown with yer. He doesn't know yer. You know that. You think I don't know, but I can see into yer head, Mal, cos you an me we're kinda like the same person. The money'll be pourin in. An the chicks'll be there, the babes.

Then I'll tell yer, so. After a few weeks like of rakin in the cash, I'll tell yer what is happenin to me exactly, an then you can adopt me or somethin. Jesus, why would you? Why would you need to adopt me, like? Amn't I your son, as good as anyways?

Then we can do all the things that boys an fathers do together. Whatever they are, like.

'My boy's comin' to see me, Brendan. From London.'

Mal's havin a pint after a day on the street. I'm in the bag.

'That's grand, Mal.'

125

'Pity it's not under better circumstances . . . '

'How old is he?'

'Fourteen . . . ' A good while then, as neither of 'em speaks. Just the floaty stream of the craic goin on behind 'em. 'Things are gonna get better, Brendan. Feel it in my water. I mean, it's a terrible shame like, that we had to be re-united by Jan's death. But I mean . . . You should have heard the young fella talkin' to me on the phone. He really wants to come. It was *his* idea.' His voice quivers with joy. 'Now don't get the wrong idea like. I'm not expectin' much at this stage. I mean we don't really know each other. Not at all.'

Floaty craic again.

'But there's gotta be somethin' there. With yer own flesh an' blood.'

'Sure there has,' replies Brendan, with a smile.

Jesus! Flesh an blood. What the fuck does *that* mean exactly? If you're the same flesh an blood you're gonna love each other? That what it means? When any fucker with a brain the size of a chicken can see that if you're the same flesh an blood, you're liable to want to kill each other before too long. Look at the papers. Look at the news. Will you just listen to yourselves?

'When's he comin'?'

'Friday.'

'Who's bringin' him?'

'Jan's husband. David.' *Law of Ssssh*. Then, 'Ah, he's alright, I suppose. I mean the break up was all very amicable you know. Jeez it's all so long ago . . . '

You fuckin liar. Tryin to pass it off as somethin that happened in another lifetime. It still hurts. It's still killin yer.

He was good to me that night. Cos he needed me for money makin. I wouldn't sleep in the bed though, cos I was scared of pissin it, an scared he might feel the wee movement of mi wooden chest or see the little wooden thing that seemed to be growin faster than Pinnochio's nose.

The next two days went by like a fast car.

Buskin. Launderette. This massive clean up at the flat. Mal had borrowed some flash new hoover from the neighbour. The roarin was wicked an I was helpin him. Can you believe that like? Buzzin around an liftin things, jumpin up an down like. We threw out tons o'crap.

I got real caught up in Mal's excitement. The whole thing. Wasn't thinkin about Joey at all. We were both completely crazy like, goin round the flat like a pair of mad dancers. Or Acrobat Scrubbers. *Weeee!* It was brilliant. Dodgin between Mal's legs with pairs o'shoes, jumpin on a chair just as the hoover came by, suckin up months o'crumbs.

Why was I helpin prepare for mi enemy's arrival? Dunno. To be honest with yer now, I didn't expect anythin to come of it. An what else could I do, like?

'Jesus, you're transformed!' Mal's in from the barbers, in his cleaned corduroy jacket. His hair's neat, an shorter. His beardy face is completely shaved.

'Whaddya think?' he says to me all nervous, taking a drag of his fag. 'I was gonna keep a moustache but I thought it made me look like a car salesman . . . '

It put the shite up me an no mistake, the way Mal was lookin like some scrubbed kid. Like he was sayin accept me please accept me. An somehow he looked less than he was. Cos the dirt an the beard an the wildness, it was all part of *him*. He looked like someone else.

Scary scary panicky.

That night there was a bottle o'the brown stuff sittin on the table, Just a wee one. 'I'm gonna take one drink, just to get me off to sleep,' he says.

'I'm just having this one more an' then I'm goin' to my bed'

'Juss one more . . . help me sleep then . . . '

'Jusss . . . *leastI'llsleeptonighteh?*"

'Joey . . . '

Sprawled out on top o'the bed like a fella that's decided to end it all an gone SPLAT from a high place. Snorin. Alarm set for 8.30.

I looked at him. Jesus what I couldn't be doin now. I could destroy everythin. I could wreck the flat. I could turn the alarm off an leave the fucker in his bed an he'd miss 'em altogether. Maybe then they'd come lookin for him an find the drunken aul bastard as he really is, turn on their heels an fly back to England.

Did I do anything of the kind? Did I fuck. Maybe I should have, all things considered.

Little Saint Lar resurrected the fuckin aul sot the minute the alarm went off.

'Do I have to breathe life into yer miself? Somebody's got to be strong an sober around here . . . ' says I, bringin him the tea, like some mammy seein her wayward son off to his first mornin at work.

An after I performed the Miracle of the Raising of Mal, you think I got any kinda thanks for it? Did I fuck. 'Now I know how Jesus feels . . . ' says I.

'Wha?'

'Nothing . . . '

'YOU FUCKIN' CUNT. IT'S A FUCKIN' CONSPIRACY! HOW THEY MAKE THESE FUCKIN' THINGS! HOW ARE THESE FUCKIN' BLADES SUPPOSED TO GO ON THIS RAZOR!'

He rages out o'the bathroom like he's comin out to fight a battle, his shirt flappin behind him.

'Fix this razor for me,' orders Mal.

'Can't do that, Mal. Sure, I'm only a puppet.'

Wrong thing to say. I'm mad, so I say the wrong thing. Sure, don't we all do that some time, let the tongue off the lead? Please don't, Mal. No, I didn't mean it!

He threw me in the press. This time it really hurt.

'That's right. Absolutely fuckin' right. A puppet is exactly what y'are.' He slams the door.

'Jesus. Why couldn't you fuckin' clip in like that to begin with?' he yells at the razor. After the shave I hear his mouth near the door o'the press. Makes it sound strange, like a fella I don't know.

'You fuckin' do anythin' divilish Lar, an I swear to you yer gonna be firewood by the end o'the week. I don't know whether Joey's comin' to the flat or whether he isn't, but anything out of order, an you've had it, ok?'

Slam. Tuctuctuctuc. Gone.

I started cryin. But this was no little tear. This was as big an as long as the river itself. At the end of it all, I blinked.

I blinked. Jesus I blinked.

I did it again like. It hurt like fuck. An again.

An somewhere somewhere was the faint flutter of a heart . . .

I opened the door o'the press. I came out. The curtains were still closed. The room was asleep. I was like a dream wanderin round the room's head.

There was a mirror screwed on to the wall by the bed like, about a foot off the floor. It must have been there when Mal moved in, cos he would never have put it there himself. He'd have had no real use for it.

I wanted to see miself close up. I dragged one o'the old white chairs from the table an stood on it. I looked at miself for a long long time before I did anythin.

I stared at mi face first. Mi eyes were wet. An there was some movement like, in mi pupils. The smile was still there as firm as ever but the hinge o'the jaw seemed smoother now, an mi varnished face gave a bit when you touched it.

I looked at one of mi handies. I took off the glove, carefully, cos they were made o' balsa wood an delicate. There was somethin like tissue paper all over them. Wrinkly, wet. Skin. I made mi hands dance before me. One would dance alone, then they'd do a duet, then they'd turn into the shadow of a bird . . . an then a rabbit an a wolf . . . I sang a little song too for them to dance to.

I was changin. Beautiful terrible beautiful terrible beautiful.

BEAUTIFUL

Terrible. Jesus it's . . .

I just went on like that for a good while, tryin to decide

whether what was happenin to me was a good thing or a bad thing, before it hit me that it was both. Like everythin. Like anythin important anyways.

I opened the shirt a bit to see if the foam that was wrapped around mi wooden chest was turnin into skin. It wasn't. The wood was turnin into skin under it.

I didn't want to look any more. Not yet.

I carefully put the gloves back. I was scared if I was too rough, I'd pull the skin away, it was that thin. I buttoned up mi shirt. Then I took a drink of milk an went back to the press. I closed the door. I was in the press where the Things go.

I mean, what was the point like? Who was I tryin to fool? Mal was throwin his arms round a nice human kid right now. His kid. Joey. An Joey was sayin, 'Dad I'm so pleased to see you. Let me live here with you forever.'

Who was I like, to compete with that? A kinda grotesque half human thing.

I wondered then what would happen like if this changin didn't stop, went on. What then? If Joey came to live here, right, then wouldn't he an I be brothers? Jesus, I'd be jealous as hell o'the little bastard. An would I be a younger or an older brother? I'm like one o'these Gods I heard about on the telly who sprung fully formed from daddy's thigh or somethin. I don't have an age.

In a flash like, I saw miself protectin Joey after Mal had drink taken. But it wasn't possible. Me an Joey together? There was somethin wrong with the picture.

All these thoughts went round like clothes in a washer, tangled an dampy. I sighed a bit, an got comfortable. I started to like that press. I was startin to feel it was where I belonged like.

Suddenly mi hands came together like magnets. Like I was prayin like. Outside the door there was the sound of somethin crossin the floor.

'Gimme them fuckin' arms back, you little bollix.'

She couldn't get in, though she banged on the door an cursed an prayed an cried, 'I must be the wickedest woman that ever was in the Christian World, to have mi arms stolen.' Then she wept

130

an begged me to come out. But Lar is no fool. He stayed put. I'll never be free of her.

After a wee while she went back to her coffin under the bed, mumblin her prayers.

I only saw Joey the one time. The day he was leavin. He came up the stairs an knocked on the door. It was open an swung on the hinges, like we was all in a horror film . . .

Do come in . . .

'Mal? Hello?'

Shipwreck

Dear Joey,

I decided to write first rather than phone you. You can say more in a letter. I don't know about you but when I'm talking on the phone I don't say anything real or deep. I don't know why. Do you understand? I'm sure you do.

I want to write about your mother, but it's hard. Tell you things about her. She was a wonderful person and you must miss her very very much. Her dying has been a terrible blow to me. That might be hard to understand as we haven't been together for a good while. But believe me when I say I loved her very much and that once, we both loved each other.

Do you know where we met? Why would you? It was Hyde Park in the summer of 82 (I don't know, maybe she's told you some of this stuff already). She was sketching a glass of water on a white table in a café. The sun caught the glass in a way that made it look alive. I was drawing some old tramp sitting by the lake, swigging back the hard stuff. And there now, I suppose, was the essence of all our problems. She was drawing something cool and sharp and clear, while I was drawing something dirty and worn.

Our meeting, well it was one of those fated things. We tumbled into each other's eyes and fell into each other's hearts. It didn't seem possible or right to ever climb out again.

Your mother helped me a lot with my work. As I'm sure you know, she had a Fine Art degree, whereas I was what people called "self-taught". That's sometimes a compliment and sometimes just a plain insult. It keeps you fresh and original, and yet it also makes you make mistakes. She lent me books, and we spent days in galleries together. Sometimes we'd fantasise that we'd get locked into the Tate say, and spend the night among the exhibits. We did actually try this once, but some terrifying security guards found us and frogmarched us out, threatening to call the cops and all manner of punishments! How we managed to convince him that we weren't art thieves, I'll never know.

All through this time, before you were born son, we were never really desperate for cash. We both had part time jobs on and off, or we were on the dole. We got by. I worked a lot for the theatres in the West End backstage which I enjoyed, and as you might just remember, stuck somewhere in a little corner of your brain that hasn't become clogged up with the schoolwork and canoeing, I also had a spot at the side of Kensington Gardens on a Sunday, where your mother and I used to exhibit and sell our paintings.

Your mother started to change. She got tired of our life, and felt it was going nowhere. She wanted a man with a steady job, who could buy her a nice house and make a secure base for you growing up. That was natural enough. I, Joey, was not that person. I simply could not be that person, without betraying myself. Can you understand that? I know what you'll say to this. 'But if you loved us . . . '

There are some things son, that are even greater than love. That cost too much. I suppose you'll be thinking I'm a selfish bastard. You might be right.

At first, I tried to be what your mother wanted. I really did try. And it was very hard for her too, because she knew all along I couldn't be that kind of person. And then I still believe that part of her actually didn't really want me to change at all. She knew herself that if I did change so we could stay together, I wouldn't be me anymore. I wouldn't be the person she fell in love with.

Because I didn't change, I had to pay. We all paid. All three of us, but the person who paid the highest was me. You and your mother got David, who is a very understanding man. I got nobody.

This makes me bitter. I suppose I've always been bitter, but this set the seal on it. And yet, looking back on it, I had no need to be so bitter because I had a choice, although it didn't look like it at the time. It was an impossible choice, but it was a choice. Yet, there's been times not so long ago, when I've wandered round my place cursing your mother rotten.

I've blamed her for years. And it was her fault. And it wasn't. Do you understand what I'm saying at all?

Now she's dead, and what is there to show for it?

You. That's what. And can I say right now that I'm very – I'm very proud of you. I hadn't seen you for a good while in the flesh. Well you're almost a man. Maybe you're embarassed that I say that – it's a bit like saying how you've grown. (and as we're talking about it you must have got your growing genes from your mother's side, because her whole family is tall and slim, and my lot aren't.) Sorry. Now I'm embarassing you.

Last time I saw you – before you came here that is – was when you were eleven, do you remember, and I was in London for a few days and we went to a museum. There was a hologram exhibit on. I tell you, I felt a bit like a hologram myself that day. I wondered whether you didn't feel like a hologram too. We didn't know what to say.

I felt the same when you were here. Did you? Of course, it was a sad time, which didn't make it any easier.

It's hard when there's a short time and the pressure's on too, well enjoy yourself. There are all kinds of things you want to say, and you're so full of all kinds of feelings, but you can't express them because you're scared they're going to tear open old wounds, and everybody's going to start crying. Then it'll be your fault you've ruined the day entirely for everyone. That was what it was like for me sometimes when I used to take you to Kensington Gardens when you were small.

So what should be like a normal holiday becomes like this trial by fire, everyone trying to be polite but feeling as if there's this river inside about to burst its banks.

Do you know what was the best moment of your whole stay here? Remember when we were all three of us on the bridge, David, then you, then me, looking out to the sea? And below us, the canoeists were trying to beat the current and paddle upstream under the bridge. You turned to me and you started talking to me about your canoeing and your badges and medals for it. and it was as if David wasn't there. There was just you and me and we'd been together all our lives. David noticed it, do you remember, and went off to get some ice cream, but as soon as he went away, you went quiet again on me, as if you were scared to be that open with me, without him being there.

Believe me, there is nothing to be frightened of from me.

I know I have no real rights over you as a father. After all, what did I do after your mother and me split up? I walked. Once David came onto the scene I didn't really feel I could stay around. That's not David's fault. It's nobody's fault. Or maybe it's everybody's fault, I don't know. The thing is, what you've got to understand is, it was nothing against you. I was so hurt. So hurt, that I just had to put the whole thing away from me. Can you understand that? Because when I was ringing you or sending you a present or anything, all I could think of was how me and your mother had gone wrong.

That was all I could think of. It was eating me inside. It still does.

I'm sorry.

As I told you the time we went off into the mountains and we were sitting outside that little pub when David went to buy us coffee or something, I wanted to come to your mother's funeral. If I'd known about it, I would definitely have been there. Please believe me.

Funny thing Joey, I was thinking. If your Mother and I had made it, then we had plans to move to Ireland. You would have had a completely different life altogether. I'm not saying better now, please believe me, just different.

Was I what you expected? That's a dangerous sort of question.

Hope I was worth the trip. I don't know how much David told you about me. Are there pictures of me at all in any photo albums? There was a portrait of your mum I'd done years and years ago in the kitchen, remember – of course that was in the old house. Maybe ask David about it.

I don't know how to end this letter, except to say, I'm planning a trip to London in the autumn when things get quieter here. I've some business to get sorted. David has said I might even come and stay with you. He is a very generous man.

If you have time in your busy schedule it'd be really nice if you'd write to me. I promise I'll write back.

I need you now. I really need you.

Love,

Mal.

Notice he didn't have the balls to sign it Dad.

There was a fair bit of crossin out, includin, 'I hope your father wasn't a disappointment to you.'

I put the letter down. Mal was out. He's always out these days.

He wrote it a week ago. Never sent it. It has big browny rings on it. Tis a beer mat now.

Take *me* Mal. I'm fuckin all you've got.

Rewind. Joey's last day in Ireland.

Joey's in the room. A tall youngfella, short dark hair, olive skin like his father. O so clean. Confident lookin. Not like the squashy thing in the picture of Never Never Land.

He's come to say goodbye. He's run up five flights o'stairs. I'm peepin out through a crack in the press.

'Mal? Hello?'

Joey looks round the room, fascinated like. He sees the Kensington Gardens picture. Smiles a little smile. As his eyes scan the room though, the smile falls off his face.

Then he sees Mal on the bed, sprawled out, like one of them deadbeats you see in some old paintings. In one hand is an almost finished half bottle, in another, the stub of a fag. There's a hole in the pillow case. Joey was lucky to find us alive I reckon.

It had been Joey's last night. Joey an David had gone off to their hotel early, Mal hadn't been able for that. Not him, he'd gone out on the piss. 'What've I got at home?' he snarls when he comes in, 'Nothing but a telly, an' a talkin' piece o'wood, which is nothin' more than fuckin' voices in my head!'

Next mornin, Mal had promised to meet them in town. When he hadn't turned up, Joey'd insisted that he wasn't goin without sayin goodbye.

He stood there lookin at Mal for a long while. Absolutely still like a statue. Then he sighed a great sigh. He wiped his hand across his face. Dropped it. Then he looked around again, but he didn't look fascinated anymore. His face closed down. Then Mal moaned. Joey looked back at him.

'Mal?'

'Uh?' Mal woke up. I think he thought he was dreamin. 'Jesus. Joey.' He sat up an smiled a bit, feelin like crap that he'd been found out.

'We were waiting for you,' says Joey, his voice shaky. His hand now was fiddlin with a watch on his other wrist.

'What's the time?' says Mal soundin surprised, amazed himself like, that he could be late for such an important cup o'coffee.

'We waited an hour.' Joey looks away. 'I didn't want to go without saying goodbye.' His voice sounds dead like.

'O'course not. Course you didn't.' Mal touches his arm. Joey moves away.

'Goodbye.' Joey doesn't know what to do like, so he puts out his hand.

Mal shakes it. Holds it. Looks for a second as if he's goin to give the kid a hug. Their eyes ooze pain.

'Dad's waiting for me. I've got to go. Bye.'

And ever so quick, Joey turns fast an slams the door which, as the lock's not on, kinda bounces back open like an invitation that

Mal doesn't take, preferrin to drown in the duvet an his own misery.

Tuctuctuctuctuctuc. Gone. Gone.

Gone but not forgotten like.

Like a whole raft o'people, Mal is a genius at buryin memories that aren't that great. That's how he could write that letter to the kid without mentionin that whole sorry episode, I suppose.

I'm makin it sound like I'm weepin buckets over all this. I was over the moon altogether. There were some dodgy moments there like, when there was a good bit o'that "bonding" as they call it on the telly, but the final few moments were a total disaster. Which is what I wanted like. I suppose.

I wanted Mal to be happy with his son Lar. Not happy with his son Joey.

As Mal sobbed away into his pillow after Joey had gone, I stayed in mi bunker thinkin about what to do next. Part o'me was feelin guilty for being so happy, so very happy, when he was so fuckin dismal, but then, what can you do?

At the moment Lar, I tried to reason with miself an shut out the sobbin an the occasional cries of 'Joey' an 'Jan' I heard from the room, you're not that well thought of at the moment, either as a Thing or a Breather. As a Thing, all I do is remind the poor bastard of his total failure as an artist. An he doesn't even know I *am* a Breather. An I'm not a Breather yet. Who's to say I might not turn back into a Thing? If I tell him at the wrong moment – it's like the final fling o'the dice. Who knows what'll happen? At the moment right, if I talk, he just thinks he's lost the plot an there's this strange voice like comin from his head. It's gettin that the only time he'll be ok with me is when he's drunk, an not always then.

Mi happiness starts to melt. I'm thinkin about how wonderful it was to be a Thing. I mean it must have been wonderful, cos you didn't have any of this shite to deal with. But then, cos I wasn't conscious, I hadn't a notion of what it *felt* like to be a Thing, cos the whole point o'being a Thing is that you don't have the feelings that Breathers have got. Do you know what I'm sayin like?

By night time Mal had shoved the incident with Joey at the flat under the bed entirely, with Peggy O'Thatch an the photo albums. Locked it away. But once in a while he'd kinda glare at me, like the whole thing was my fault. He didn't speak to me at all. He scared me.

We started to work like fuck again in the River of People. *Diddlyfuckineye*. The summer would soon be over like, an then we'd really be swimmin in shite. An everythin seemed to move faster when we were on the street like, as if you'd speeded up the video.

O'course when you shove yer dirty knickers under the bed, tis alright for a day or two, an then the fuckers start to smell. At first, when Mal was in the pub, he'd be high as a kite, tellin everybody what a great success his meetin with Joey had been an what a great kid he was an how the years had kinda just melted away an how he was plannin to go off to visit him in the autumn.

They all said grand grand but they musta seen like, they musta known that it all wasn't as rosy as he was paintin it, an nobody asked any questions like, they just all said grand. I tried to work this out like. I mean, why didn't they say somethin? Why did they let him get deeper an deeper into this illusion? Was it cos they felt sorry for him? Didn't want to hurt his feelings? Was it –

Jesus! Or was it just fuckin easier like? Was it just easier to say grand to the poor fucker's face, then all shake their heads together an say poor Mal when he'd staggered out the door? Tis cosy enough then to cuddle together an feel sorry for him, suppin yer pints in yer common humanity! Jeez it makes me so mad!

After a few days o'this the Good Ship Joey started takin on

the water very fast, Mal started takin on the porter, an the final meetin between the kid an himself started stinkin the place out.

Through all this, I played a low low profile. That way our place was like a simmerin pot, instead of a boilin pot which is what it would have been if I'd been openin an closin mi gob. Most o'the time Mal was contented with this, but every so often like he'd say somethin to me, an I'd just ignore him, then I'd end up in the fuckin press anyways with mi aul friends the bag an broom. I couldn't be a Thing or a Talkin Thing or a Real Kid either.

An I was puttin off the Big Moment when I was gonna tell Mal what was happenin.

Have you ever tried not to blink? Or had to eat an drink an piss in secret? I started worryin about when I was gonna start shittin as well, an what was gonna happen if I had an accident, an how the fuck was I gonna explain *that* away. Mi body was startin to feel kinda alien, kinda like this strange thing like, that I didn't know . . .

Apple wood, holly wood, mahogany an balsa . . . .

This is what a pupa feels, I think.This is what it feels like to turn into a butterfly. Squeezin out from this pod of spit an skin. Gaspin. Butterflies only live for one day, right? I heard that on the telly, I think . . . But it's a beautiful day an the butterfly looks lovely.

It looks lovely.

Does the butterfly know how long it has?

Jesus, I'm gonna get sick. I'm gonna get human an get sick. I'm gonna be knocked down by a car or somethin an be rushed into casualty an all these people are gonna be hangin over me, rushin around with machines an thumping mi little chest an screaming 'Jesus kiss o' life, 500 mls *o'streptofuckincyanide!*'

God help me!

God. I'm gonna have to think about God. I'm gonna have to

decide. Is there God or isn't there . . . I'm gonna have to decide. What subjects do I like at school? What are mi hobbies like? What am I gonna to be when I grow up? How many points do I need to get into Third Level? What do I want to do? Jesus I don't know . . . . Somebody help me. Do I like girls? What kinda girls? Easy girls? Good girls? What? What colour hair? What kinda shape do I like? Do I like fellers too? FUCK OFF! Jesus I might like. Anythin could happen . . . I'm at sea. On the ocean . . . Like Mal. An how'm I gonna make a livin? No more dancin in the streets for a real kid. The guards'd be on you in no time. Help me. Jesus, I've not a livin soul to turn to. Help me!

So all this is spinnin round in mi head an Mal's sinkin to the bottom of the sea. Isn't it just great to be alive?

The phone rings about a week later. I'm in the Press Residence. Lucky for Mal he hadn't set sail as yet . . .

It's David.

'David, How are yer?'

'I'm fine, Mal, how are you?'

'Is Joey there?'

'No, he's out at canoeing practise.'

'Oh, right.' Mal sinks a bit. Takes a deep breath, then, 'You know I was so sorry not to have been able to see you off properly as we'd planned. I had a business appointment that night. It went on till late. I overslept.'

'Oh, I see . . .' said David, goin along with it.

'Did Joey not tell you that?'

'No. He didn't tell me anything.'

'Jesus, David. I told him to give you my apologies. Poor kid, he must have been wrecked by the whole thing.'

'I think so.'

A thick pause. Mal strikes a match.

'To tell you the truth, Mal, I wish I hadn't brought him really.'

'Don't be saying that, David.' Suck in the smoke.

'Maybe it was too soon. I dunno. I mean at first he seemed to be really enjoying it, and as you know, it was *him* that pressed to come. But he's said very little about it since we got back. I asked him whether he wanted to ring you or send you a letter or something. He just said no, and started talking about something else. So I thought I'd better leave it for a bit.'

'Oh.'

'I mean, look I rang to ask, so I'm going to,' says the voice of David, determined. 'What was going on in your place when Joey came up? I mean, you didn't have a woman up there, did you?'

'I did not,' said Mal, very rattled.

'I'm sorry, Mal, I'm only asking because I'm baffled. You know me, I'll do what the boy wants. I love Joey. He isn't my son but he could as well be. If he wants to have some contact with his natural father, then fine –'

Mal starts pantin a bit.

' – but I can't force him.'

'O'course. O'course, you're great,' says Mal, with a thick slice o'sarcasm under his rasher of humility. 'I'll write. I'll write him a letter.'

'Do that.'

'I will.'

'Bye.'

'Bye bye.' *Clunk*

'IF HE WANTS TO HAVE SOME CONTACT WITH HIS NATURAL FATHER, THEN THAT'S FINE???' yells Mal at the phone when the call was done, 'Let me tell yer, yer fuckin' bollox, I could get this kid in no time. I could drag yer through the fuckin' courts. He is *my* blood! So nice, so fuckin nice! Who the fuck do yer think you are?'

He starts wreckin the flat, screamin an shoutin more o'the same, an I tell yer, do I feel glad to be in the Press Residence.

SLAM. *Tuctuctuctuctuc.* Gone.

When Mal was around those times, I felt how a small wild beast must be feelin all the time. Always on the edge, never knowin

142

what was gonna jump out at yer an leave nothin but yer innards for the crows. When he went away, I felt like I was lyin on a nice soft bed.

For Mally was out there juss drownin in sorrows.

Not givin a shite for todays or tomorrows.

Then from under the bed I heard the cawin of Peggy, demandin her arms. I drowned her out with a cookery programme, an after that, some film about the future.

Even without Mal there, I was waitin to be jumped on.

Next day Mal was still away. I wasn't worried at first, it'd happened once or twice before, like. To be honest now, I was glad.

I was watchin this programme on the telly where this woman was talkin about the change of life. The two puppetpeople who own the fake livin room the woman's sittin in, are noddin like they know absolutely every single fuckin thing there is to know.

An I thought, that's me. That's me. I'm going through a change of life like. That's all it is. Chill, as they say. Everyone changes, an you've just gotta take it as it comes.

This satisfied me for exactly one minute by the kitchen clock, then I started yellin at the telly, the way Mal yelled at the razor. Except that in my case the puppetcouple started to talk back to me.

'You fuckin' arseholes!' I yells. 'Whaddyou know about life?'

'That's the pot calling the kettle black, I must say. You're just a Thing, Noddy,' says She. He looks down at his fingernails.

'Just ignore him Linda,' says the fella under his breath.

'No Charles, I won't ignore him,' She says with her big smily shield an swordy eyes. 'Who do you think you are, disturbing our sense of what's real and what isn't real?'

I was about to ask her what the fuck did that *mean* like, but She went on.

'I mean you don't expect anyone to take you seriously, do you?'

143

'You fuckin bitch,' I spit back. I'm sorry like. I couldn't answer her, so the abuse just came tumblin out.

'I mean, who is going to buy the idea of a piece of wood turning into a person?' The way She said that would have made every tree give up reachin for the sky an crash to the ground.

'Sometimes, you aul biddy, the truth is harder to buy than lies!' says I, tryin to sound like some kinda hero in a movie, where the fella's gotta mission to tell the world a great truth.

'Perhaps you'd like to share this with the viewers?' says Charley, with a snarly smile. His hand shoots out o'the telly –

'Get off me, you bollox!'

– An he tries to grab me an pull me into Tellyworld.

'Come on now . . . come on . . . ' I'm fightin best I can, grabbin onto the leg o'the armchair.

'Let's have a big hand now for Lar, who thinks he's turning into a human boy, ladies and gentleman!' says She, an all the little puppetpeople watchin her just clap an clap.

'I'm not goin!'

'Come on now, don't be shy!' The hand makes another grab, an this time he has me.

'Come on you wooden prick, this is your chance!' She hisses.

On the floor by the chair there's the remains of a plate o'chips that Mal brought in, an a big greasy fork. I grab it, so I'm only holdin onto the chair with one hand. Charles takes his chance, an pulls me toward the screen. I give his manicured handie a mighty stab!

'YOU LITTLE BASTARD!' he screams. The giant hand shoots back into the screen.

'YOU can't use that kinda talk! You're on the telly!' says I, laughin mi hat off.

Off with the set. Ha ha. Ha ha. Beat the fuckers. Beat 'em. Beat 'em. I'm lookin around for Peggy O'Thatch. *Panicky panicky.*

Where's Mal?

Tick tock tick tock. What's gonna happen if Mal doesn't come back? I can't live without him, what'll I do? *Tick tock.* I can't make money without him. *Tick*. I need him. *Tock*. Where'd I go? *Tick tock*. How'd I move about? *Tock*. What about the giant boys who hang round on the stairs? *Tock*.

So fuckin amazin I am to be sure, but I'm helpless.

I finished off the pack o'wood shavings an had mi first shite. It hurt. It really hurt. I fell right in an very nearly drowned.

Tick tock.

The room is closin in. Maybe it's tryin to hold me, comfort me like, say don't go away, or maybe it's tryin to tell me that it's gonna be mi coffin an it'll never let me go.

Tick tock.

I climb up to the sink, get a small drink o'water. It doesn't hurt so much to drink anymore.

There's a terrible rattlin under the bed. I know what it is. When I turn from the sink, she's standin there, looking all woeful at me.

'Gimme mi arms . . . ' an now not a banshee's wail, but a cry that comes from a terrible need.

'Peggy,' I say, all quiet, like I know somethin all of a sudden. 'I am so close to a real boy now, there's no way you can have mi arms. Skin an bone is useless to yer. You want wood an fabric.'

An she stares at me with her little black button eyes for what feels like forever, swayin like a reed. Then she totters back to the bed, an the shoebox coffin. 'I curse yer . . . Keep yer arms. You've nothin' that I want. But you won't forget me, I'll tell yer that . . . '

Peggy O'Thatch is gone.

Tick tock. The giant cranes move against the sky. *Tick tock*. Mal, where are yer, Mal? *Tock*.

Maybe he joined the ranks o'suicides that jump into the river.

Ha. I can see 'em all now, havin this great party. Mostly youngones. Jeez the room is like a vault an it's packed. They're havin this really gas time talkin over a few jars about what shitey lives they had on the earth, how nobody really noticed there was anythin the matter, or if they did, they didn't give a fuck about it.

The party fades away in mi head.

Tick.

The clock stops.
Fuck. The clock stopped.

The sky's red an Mal comes in. He looks well battered, mouth cut an a black eye comin. His sheepskin coat is like a pack o'wolves have been at it. He doesn't look at me.

I'm so glad to see him like. But I'm mad too. An scared. 'How are yer?' I squeak.

Nothing.

'Mal?'

'How are yer?' It's like a growl, but I'm so grateful for it like, so grateful, it's like he patted me on the head, or stroked mi face or somethin. He's just standin in the middle o'the room. Lookin ahead. I lift mi arm up slow an put mi hand in his. He still doesn't look at me. I think better of it an move mi hand away. Maybe it's better he doesn't look at me. He won't see mi tears then.

Then he turns to me suddenly.

'Did anyone ring?'

'No.' What he means is, did Joey ring?

Did Joey ring? Well the truth is, you bag o'fuckin skin that the kid from Kensington did phone yer last night an guess what? Yours truly took the call. an he said to me, 'Is my daddy there?' An I said, 'He is not, you fuckin little bollox, you missed yer chance. You could have got him for yerself when you came over the water, but you blew it entirely. All because you saw him drunk, just cos you saw the real Mal, not the one he tried to show yer, an you couldn't take it. Just cos a drop of porter an a few nights out doesn't figure in the life of a boy from Kensington, who's probably only happy when he's flyin round with the fuckin fairies in the park, you lost him. You fuckin lost him!'

I didn't say that. I didn't say it, but I could have done. Joey didn't ring anyways.

Mal smiled at me. He smiled at me.

Tell him. Tell him now.

146

'Mal?'

'Come on, Lar. Into the bag with you. Mr Bendy's got a brilliant destination for us this time.' His voice is soft an encouragin like.

He doesn't need to ask again. I leap into the arms of Nike. Things are pickin up. They're pickin up!

As we pass the bed, I hear the needy voice o'Peggy O'Thatch. 'Mi arms!'

'See you later Peggy . . . ' I call back, all happy like.

'Ha. You won't be needin' 'em where *you're* goin', little bollix – '

SLAM. *Tuctuctuctuctuc* Gone.

Lost

Skin's itchy itchy under the foam.

Where are we goin Mal, where are we goin? I can hear the power an the rush o'the river beneath us. We've stopped. We've stopped on the bridge. An though I see nothin cos I'm in the bag, I can see in mi head Mal starin down the river an out to the Sea, starin into the great promise of Beyond, when you're nothin again, just a bit o'the ocean. An Mr Sun's sayin, 'I'm goin' down, so why don't you do the same?'

'D'you think, 'says the redfaced ball, 'it's a laugh goin' up an down all the time like, seeing you miserable feckers? I tell you it isn't. One day I'm gonna go down an' never come up again, an' that'll serve you right, you bastards.'

People passin passin all the time. What's the craic, *Ciao bello,* howzitgoin, are yer gonna see her again, fuck off you. *Howie take the camera, will ya.*

I get this horrible feelin Mal is gonna jump an take me with him. Don't jump. Or if you *do* jump leave me on the fuckin pavement will yer, an I can be just like the Killer Doll an be in a million sequels. *I don't wanna die, not now.* I am alive. I AM ALIVE.

Suddenly, I'm all ragin inside me. Mad, cos *he* thinks it's ok to kill us both. Why don't *you* jump, you fucker? Fuckin jump an leave me. If that's what you want like. Don't worry about me. I'll make it ok. Isn't life fuckin hard enough? Haven't I got enough of mi own fuckin shite to carry without havin to carry your crap as well? I don't need yer. I'll be free.

Shit, is that true like, will I make it, can I make it without Mal?

No. If Mal dies, I'll die. I know that like. *I won't die.* Mi chest is movin now. *I'm alive.* I'm not the same as Mal. I'm me. *Me.* I have mi own life. Not true, bollox. You're still a puppet. Most of yer is still made of wood. An then you're only 30 inches high. No Breather is 30 inches high unless you're a kid like. An you're not growin, are yer? You'll live to be a hundred an still be 30 inches high.

'Y'ok in there?' Mal spoke to me. Mi heart jumped. He opened Nike's lips, an peeped in. His face was flushed an he was sweatin a bit.

'I . . . Sure, I'm grand,' I whispered back, in case there was someone around..

An without another word we started travellin an left the river to her own mad decision. Into the town.

How are ye I'm grand. Text me back then, will yer? Fancy a pint? Fiddle de Dee an Bodhran . . .

Pneumatic drill punches the pavement, drownin out everythin.

'Do them fellas never stop?' a young girl shouts to her friend.

Mal's walkin fast. Bang the bag goes against the wall. Voices cracklin, passin.

How are ye?

I'm feelin hot. Hot. Tis the foam. Mi skin under the foam. Jesus. I'm wrigglin in the bag.

'Keep still will yer? They'll think I've some kind of an animal in there.'

Oh Jesus Jesus . . . Do what Mal says do . . .

Black. Get the feelin it's been that way for a good while. Open mi eyelids. Still black. But I'm breathin. Suffocatin. Air. Jesus give me air. Open the zip just a bit like. Come on please. God, open yer mouth you fuckin plastic coffin.

Air. We're in a car. I'm at Mal's feet. Two faces juttin out like two birds of prey above me. Mal's chewin somethin. The reddyfaced driver's eatin a sandwich.

'Carmel always makes me sandwiches when I've a long day ahead o'me.'

An he's tellin Mal about his kids an how they're so ungrateful an won't give a hand with the business, though they've been reared with death like, not like him who was a farmer who grew up rearin cows, an came late to the funeral business. So ungrateful, considerin death has put the food on their plates an helped pay for their education.

Fuck, we're in a fuckin hearse. We turn off the road.

'I wonder if you couldn't help me now,' says the fella to Mal.

Mal looks at him, worried.

'Thing is, Mrs O'Flaherty's just died. Tom O'Flaherty, the husband, he knew she was gonna die well enough. For months! An didn't I tell him to make a bed up for her in the parlour, so that when she did pass on, we would not have to carry the remains down the very narrow stairs, to lay her out in the coffin.'

'Sorry?'

'Especially as Mrs O'Flaherty – well not to speak ill o'the dead, but she was rather a large woman . . . You'd be doing me a great turn now if you could give me a hand.'

'To carry the body?'

'Got it in one. Mr O'Flaherty's not a young man, he has a heart condition, an my back is playin' me up something terrible.'

Mal said nothin, just stared at the fella's face, an old apple past its best.

'Good man. Mighty,' says the Apple, 'Let me do the talkin' now. Have you ever handled a corpse before?' They walk through the muddy yard, to the stone-faced old man at the door.

Black. I'm back home. Peggy O'Thatch has a cleaver. She's chasin me round the room an howlin the rosary, an then . . . 'Let me clean, let me pray!' Mi arms start clappin together, like they're not my arms, an I'm going, 'No No No!'

'Look – will yer – please,' I says weepin, 'Please I'm a person now . . . '

'Yer a bollix!'

'Look at mi arms.' says I, pullin back the little shirt an jacket, 'Will you believe your own eyes? Do you see the skin? Do you?'

She raises the cleaver up. Black.

Dreamin. Standin in a great big field. There's this feelin right, that somethin really amazin's gonna happen. Mal's standin behind me, an the diddlyeye's goin an I'm dancin. Then all of a sudden two tenners float down from the sky, into the bag in front of us. Suddenly the field's full o'people. Slowly at first, then more an more an more. It starts rainin money on 'em. They're all lookin up to the sky, like little birdies waitin for the worms. An everybody goes mental pickin it all up, an dancin an laughin an washin in money, an it's such a gas like, that nobody can kinda go an spend anythin, cos they're too busy pickin it up. Then you can't see the field anymore, cos it's all just covered in notes. Everyone's laughin their hats off.

'That's mine!' A small man in a suit jabs at some woman for takin a note that didn't belong to her an before you know it, they're fightin. Everyone's fightin, an the air's thick with the money. Black.

Cold air knifes the bag. Mi head is out of it, an mi arms, like I'm in a small boat like. I'm lookin towards the ocean. We're on a cliff, very high up. Mal's sittin beside me. He's lookin out to the ocean too. An smokin. Singin an old song about America.

The tide like the slow in out of the earth breathin, far away like. Far below. Gulls nestle in the armpits of cliffs, then slide along the edge of a wind. An the great red sun's ready to snuggle down under the watery duvet. Sure, wasn't it a moment ago I was by the river at home, watchin the sun go down? Where has the time gone? Not dreamin now.

I blink. Mal sees me.

Blink. Mal watches. Says nothin at all. An I say nothin miself like. Cos there's nothin to say. There's just the old in out of the ocean, an the gulls gassin.

For a second there, I think about all the times I'd pressed the rewind, an played an replayed the scene when I told Mal what was happenin to me. Him takin it badly, throwin me away. Or him cryin with joy, holdin me to him. How I was gonna use that moment to get what I wanted, an say –

'I'm a real fuckin' kid now, an you can't treat me that way any more, Mal . . . Don't worry about Joey. *I'm* your kid. I'll be the perfect kid. I'll be everythin you ever wanted . . . '

But the truth of it, the plain truth of it was that this was how he found out. Lookin out onto the ocean, battered an tired, neither of us knowin what the fuck was goin on at all like. Both of us just lost an confused an empty. An somehow like, at peace. Cos it was a relief.

An I knew then I'd made the whole turnin into a person thing, like the answer to a prayer. Like it is in Pinocchio. Truth was, twas like a door from one dark room into another dark room which was just a bit different.

I smiled. Black again.

I open mi eyelids. Slow slow. Tis almost dark now. Still on the cliff. I'm lyin on the ground. Like a sacrifice, spread out like, greeny flames all round me, an all mi clothes are off me. The foam's lyin by me, slit open, like a soft shell. an mi chest is like the tender red skin of a new born kid. It smooths down to the dark mahogany of mi hips. All mi limbs are different colours, cos I was made of all these different woods. The grain on mi arms is almost gone an the leather elbows have smoothed entirely to velvety skin. Skin has grown across the joint of mi jaw. I can feel a small movement in mi lips. I'm cold.

There's a pain in mi back. Mal's taken out the hooks where the strings were attached. I know there's blood seepin into the soil. The cross an the strings are lyin on the grass.

Mal watches me, smokin, an drinkin from a half bottle. Watchin. Then lookin away.

'Mal, I'm cold,' I say, all weak.

He ignores me, an I start thinkin like jeez, he's turnin it round in his head, what he's gonna do with me . . . an I'm thinkin, now I'm a human now right. I've got rights, haven't I? But rights mean nothin when it's just you an this cracked thing an swoopy gulls on a high cliff before the biggest ocean in the world. Mi back hurt. I was weak. Too weak.

'What you gonna do with me, Mal?'

'Dunno, Lar.'

Law of Ssssh.

An suddenly liquid flows from mi body. From every hole. From mi eyes comes tears. Water from mi ears, sick stuff from mi mouth, piss from mi thing, hot water from behind, blood from the holes in mi back where the hooks had been. An tis like all these juices are Life itself, an I'm like this pipe ok, an they're all goin through it from one end to the other . . .

Then Mal says sadly – 'This is what life is like, my friend.'

I remember seein this Bible story on the telly about how God had asked this fella Abraham to kill his kid Isaac, who he'd had no end o'trouble bringin into the world. They were on a mountain. An he was goin to do it like, an then God stopped him. An I was waitin for a big bright light in the sky an God partin the cloudy curtains to say, 'Will you hold on a minute there, Mal . . . !'

But God didn't peep through the clouds.

The juices stopped pourin out after a few minutes.

Mal stands. He picks me up. I'm shakin. I wriggle a bit like, but there's no strength left in me, not at all, I start with the tears again. 'Don't cry now, Lar,' he says an holds me for a second like you would a baby. I cry even more. Comfort. Comfort. Tis the most perfect moment you could wish for.

He's cryin too. Please water me with yer tears . . .

Then his face turns twisty like he's smelled a bad smell. 'This isn't happenin' to me . . . it isn't happenin' . . . !' An his whole body starts writhin like he's a cloth an God is wringin him out . . . He's holdin mi leg with one hand, an he starts screamin an cryin himself . . . God help me.

'What is the matter with me? What's the matter with me?' he sobs.

'No, Mal no! Please Jesus . . . '

'SHUT THE FUCK UP WILL YER! YOU'RE A VOICE IN MY HEAD!'

An he's swingin me backwards an forwards.

'Joey, my son! MY SON!'

'Mal, please I'm real, Listen to me. Please . . . '

'*I CAN HEAR NOTHING!* NOTHING!'

He's swingin me like he's gonna throw me over the side, an I'm screamin a high pitched scream . . . which makes him scream an we're both screamin an the sound must be terrible.

The edge of the cliff. We're both jumpin, right. I can handle that. I can. You can't. I can. An if the wind had come just then, well over we would have gone right there, off to oblivion together.

Then he steps back again. Opens Nike. Throws in the cross an the strings an the clothes an finally, me too. Throws me in. *Zzzzzip.*

'You never spoke to me, Lar, it was all in mi head . . . '

We're walkin away from the edge.

Thankyou God or somebody – whoever. Another chance. Another chance to get mi strength back, then I can leave Mal like, leave him an we'll both get on with our own lives. I'll grow up. I'll get it together alright. I will. I mean, what the fuck did Pinocchio do? Jeez he can't have been more than a teenager himself when Gepetto kicked the bucket an then what happened? Still, Gepetto did have a business alright, so I suppose the kid could – but what if aul Pinoke was crap at the toymakin? What could he do then? What? Jesus he'd probably become a film director, why wouldn't he? – Jesus what am I chattin about? Pinocchio was a film. A cartoon. Pictures. I'm talkin about him as if he was –

Why've we stopped walkin?

Falling

Fallin. I'm fallin forever.

Notmuchofalifelike BREATHE *notmuchofabreathinlifeouttosea* I'm goin *outtosea* –

OJesus. Hedidit. *Mayyourotinhellanmayyerfuckindiediddlyeye.*

How are yer? I'm grand.

Whasthecraichowzitgoin?

Fuckin threw me over the edge

An I curse yer fuckin Son an God for not peepin through the clouds.

BREATHE breathe breathe, an Peggy o'Thatch an Philip the Deadbeat an Philip the Deadbeat's dog an David an Brendan an the fairy people. An I curse yer mother an father an sister an yer whole family –

An everyone who knows me.

Water's comin in Jesus water. JESUS HELP ME. How could he do this to me, he could see I was alive. Couldn't he see I was alive? This is murder now.

I'm alive. I didn't even want to be afuckinlive before, an now I've got used to the idea I'm gonna die. Let me be swallowed like the whale, like Pinoke. Let me find mi real father in that whale. Save him like in the story –

156

This is not a fairy tale. Nothin happens like it does in fuckin fairy stories. It does it does not it does doesn't does . . .

What kind of a father are yer, bollox? You're not a father. You couldn't be a father to your own *fleshanbludkid* so what a fuckin fool I was to ever expect – to think to think.

Please no . . . Why won't the fuckin zip open? That's the reality alright, that's it. Not savin yer daddy from a whale, but tryin to escape from some sweaty aul bag full o'holes.

Jesus I'm drownin. I'm gonna die. You fuckin bastard, Mal. I'm gonna . . .

Reflection

I stare at mi face sometimes in the mirror for hours.

It's brilliant.

How just with a touch of a thought like, an the smallest movement, eyes turned away, slight tilt o'the head, you can make the whole face like a beacon of feelings. Or sometimes you can be doin nothing, just starin in, down the well of yer own eyes, an the sun'll just light yer face up an you're transformed totally.

I'm wearin runners an a track suit thing that says – "New York University." While I was in the ocean I grew about a foot and a half.

Where's Mal?

They think I'm about eight. I have a proper birthday now. We decided it was next week.

I lie on the bed. In mi bedroom. Look out the window onto a concrete garden. Not far away a giant metal birdie stands watch. That giant crane probably helped to build this house.

On the walls there's pictures of hurling an football an all that craic. Tryin to make me feel at home. I put up mi first poster today. A poster of a whale.

I did it to please 'em. They were all smiles after I'd told them what I wanted to do like, an Donal came an helped me with it. He held it straight on the wall, an I tore off the bits o'tape an stuck the whale on the wall.

I wonder where Mal is now?

I stare at this spaceship on mi wallpaper an wish I was on it.

I had mi fifteen minutes of fame, but I missed it miself altogether. They found me washed up on a beach. I have the bit from the paper. They thought I was dead like. But I was alive.

I remember hearin echoey voices. Bein examined in the hospital. 'There's something terrible happened to this child . . . Look at his skin, his hips. They're a different colour to his legs an chest. an there's paint on his face. an then there's his clothes,' says this whispery woman.

'Some fucking pervert –' growlyman voice.

'Maybe he was going to a fancy dress party,' says this other very matteroffact voice.

'And he jumped into the bag, and threw himself into the ocean o'course,' sneered growlyman.

I must have had every test known to medical science when I was in that hospital, an do you know they found not a thing wrong with me. More than that, they found me completely normal. There were no bits o'wood where there shoulda been organs or joints. Mi whole body was by this time covered in skin, even though as they said like, it still had the colour of different pieces o'wood.

It was like I kinda needed the ocean to finish the job to make me into a human. I heard someone say once that we humans, we was made up of somethin like 80 per cent water. So perhaps gettin thrown into the water was just what I was waitin for. Probably why I grew such a lot.

Nothin to do with fuckin fairies an wishin on a star an all that bollox an rescuin mi daddy from the belly of the whale.

Not at all.

I didn't say a word like, for ages, no matter how many kind fellas an friendly ladies they put me with, sittin me in little rooms with lots o'stupid dolls to play with. If you picked somethin up like, you felt the eyes o'the world were on yer, makin somethin of it.

159

The truth is, I was just completely overcome like. I mean, your father doesn't try to kill yer every day. Does he?

A breeze makes the curtains roll like a wave. The giant crane growls outside the window.

A real boy. I'm a real boy. Like Joey.

Everybody was kinda convinced like, well, that someone had been doing some serious interferin with me. Sometimes I felt like they almost wanted it to be so, so it kinda explained things.

There *was* foul play alright, but not the kinda foul play they was thinking of. There were still wounds in mi back, from the hooks where the strings went. They clearly thought like I was the victim of some very shady rituals.

'Fuck off,' I says quietly, one day. The first words I spoke after Mal tried to kill me. I said 'em to this youngone called Helen, with a kindly face an bubbly blond hair. A lot more language was to follow over the next few weeks, which o'course made 'em believe the worst. They couldn't decide how old I was at all.

Well what could I do like? I couldn't stay silent for ever. I had to weigh the whole thing up. The only way to get out o'there was to start talkin. But I had to pretend I had amnesia which only made 'em ask more questions. I mean how do yer answer questions like – 'What was your mammy like?' 'Dunno. Me mammy was a sports bag.'

They also thought, I heard 'em say, that I was from some really backward place, cos I talked kinda old fashioned. Sure I wanted to say, have you never met a leprechaun before? I'm not exactly of the twenty first century, now am I?

Where's Mal?

Jeez what the fuck do I care? He can fuckin rot in hell . . . Bet he's with Joey right now, skippin an dancin through Kensington Gardens.

He is not. Joey doesn't want him. Why would he? Why would anyone want a loser like Mal?

Me.

Why couldn't things stay as they were? Why are people never satisfied?

An I'm thinkin like, well for Pinocchio this would be a fuckin heavenly endin but for yours truly, tis anythin but. Lookin around this kid's bedroom I'm sittin in, *my* bedroom, I'm wonderin will I ever forget mi life before this? Cos there's part o'me wants to forget it so bad. It'd make startin from now so easy. An rememberin makes mi life from now so hard. I remember hearin some auldone in a pub talkin to Mal, sayin how people often forgot what it was like to be a kid, cos it was too painful to remember.

But there's part o'me wants to remember, that doesn't want to forget. That'll never forget. Cos that's me.

All the bad things, everythin. They're all me. Whether I like it or not. But as they say in best telly tradition, now I've got to pick up the pieces of mi life an go on.

Tap tap tap on the door.

'Are you ok in there, Larry?'

'I am, thanks . . . ' I don't recognise mi voice. High an sweet. Like a kid.

'Would you like a cup of tea?'

'Yes, please.'

'How do you feel after your physio today?' I'm goin to physio cos mi joints are stiff.

'Grand.'

Donal an Lynn, they're really kind. He works for a communications company an she does some kinda healin with smelly oils.

But even if they decided to adopt me like, they've got this adopted daughter Shelley, I mean *they* can't be mi parents. I mean, I am not gonna belong, am I? I am never ever gonna belong. Cos always at the back o'mi mind like, there's gonna be this other life, which I can never ever tell 'em about. Maybe if I wrote it down.

They'd think I made it up. And maybe that'd be just as well. People believe what they wanna believe. Don't they?

Will I ever see Mal again?

The bollox'll probably be cacklin with the winos by the river. Or beggin or somethin. What a sorry end.

Serve the bastard right.

An I'll be walkin past, an Donal an Lynn they'll be holdin mi hands if I let 'em, an givin me swings. We'll all be laughin our heads off. You'll put yer bottle down an look round, like you'll kind of know mi laugh somehow, even though it sounds way different now from what it did when I was just yer wooden boy. An our eyes'll meet just for a second, an I'll see that look pass over yer eyes an I'll look away, a happy kid with happy parents facing the future with a smile.

The sun goes in. The room goes gloomy. A knock at the door. 'Will you come down and have your cup of tea with us, Larry?'

'OK. In a minute.'

'That's fine.'

The sun pops out again. I roll miself off the bed. I stretch miself up. An I feel the life flowin through me. An it feels brilliant. An I wonder whether Mal ever felt like this at all, if there was ever a time when he really felt the power of life goin right through him, an if he did, how is it possible that he could end up as he did?

Cos feelin that magic flowin through me, well it's everythin, it makes everythin ok. For now, anyways.

End

In the swelling city, The Puppetman no longer performed for the River of People, who sailed on their smiles.

He had believed that the puppet had spoken to him for a while. Now the spell had been broken.

For the Puppetman was plucked from the black foamy ocean by Catherine O'Hanlon, a rich American widow with a face as tight as a drumskin, whose daughter had seen the Man's exhibition. The Widow owned a converted castle, and asked the Puppetman to paint four landscapes from the roof, one in each direction, to hang in her Boston apartment.

The Man agreed, provided he could have money in his pocket first, and go to England and visit his Son.

And there was a coldness in the eye of the Puppetman as he walked towards the station, past the Man with his Head in a Bucket, past the Clown with the Bellhung Umbrella, past the Statue Man, past the Dark Men with Brass Instruments.

He looked down the street, then above the roofs of the shops and houses, and he thought he saw all the giant cranes lowering their heads.

Bowing down to him.

End

Other Titles from

Wynkin
deWorde

*All of our lives are unique explorations through
uncharted landscapes of experience and emotion.*

*Kerrigan, the eponymous hero of this novel,
has been flattened many times in this journey,
but in re-awakening, re-emerging in the place of his
heart - the beating heart that is Copenhagen - the
contours of his pain, his joy and his salvation bubble up
and become almost palpable on the pages of
this magnificent novel.*

ISBN: 0-9542607-1-6   450 PAGES   FICTION